COPY 62

j398.2   JEWETT, Eleanore Myers
          WHICH WAS WITCH? Tales of ghosts and
          magic from Korea. Illustrated by Taro
          Yashima. New York, Viking, 1953. 160p.
Related ⎫ illus. 2.94
Books in ⎪ 1. TALES, KOREAN 2. FOLK-LORE - KOREA
Catalog ⎬
Under   ⎭
        * Ages 9 - 12.

                              Title.   0 64

Which Was Witch?

TALES OF GHOSTS AND MAGIC FROM KOREA

Which Was Witch?

TALES OF GHOSTS AND MAGIC FROM KOREA

BY ELEANORE M. JEWETT
Illustrated by Taro Yashima
New York · THE VIKING PRESS · 1959

Copyright 1953 by Eleanore Myers Jewett

Published by The Viking Press in September 1953

Published on the same day in the Dominion of Canada
by The Macmillan Company of Canada Limited

Second printing August 1954

Third printing March 1956

Fourth printing August 1959

Fifth printing July 1961

Sixth printing June 1963

Printed in the U.S.A. by Vail-Ballou Press

This book

is dedicated with my love

to

Raymond Chester Gosda

whose interest in the Korean people

led to my writing it

CONTENTS

Which Was Witch?

TALES OF GHOSTS AND MAGIC FROM KOREA

1. WHICH WAS WITCH?

THERE was once a wise and learned man named Kim
Su-ik. He lived just inside the south gate of Seoul but
he might as well have lived anywhere for all the thought he

11

gave the matter. His mind was entirely taken up with study and books, and one could say of him, as Im Bang said of another scholar, "He used to awake at first cockcrow, wash, dress, take up his book and never lay it aside. On his right were pictures, on his left were books, and he happy between. He rose to be a Prime Minister."

One night Kim Su-ik was absorbed in studying a Chinese classic when he suddenly felt hungry. He clapped his hands to summon a servant, and immediately the door of his room opened.

His wife stepped in.

"What does the master of the house desire?" said she.

"Food," he answered briefly, his attention already returned to the book in his lap.

"I have little in the house but a few roasted chestnuts. If that will suffice I will bring them to you myself. The servants have long since gone to their sleeping quarters."

Kim Su-ik grunted his approval and went on with his studies. In a very short time the door opened again and his wife came in bearing a brass bowl full of hot roasted chestnuts. He helped himself to one and was in the act of putting it into his mouth when once more the door opened and in stepped his wife with a brass bowl full of hot roasted chestnuts.

But his wife was already there, standing beside him with the bowl in her hands!

Kim Su-ik, his mouth still open and a chestnut half in it, looked in astonishment from one to the other of the identical women. They were as like as two pins—faces, features, figures, clothes, the way they stood, the way they used their fingers and moved their shoulders. Never were twins more completely alike. Kim Su-ik passed his hands before his eyes. He must have overdone his studying, he thought to himself, read too late and too steadily. His eyes were playing tricks on him, that was all. He was seeing double.

But when he looked again the two women were still there, and what was stranger still, they seemed not to be aware of each other, but stood quietly, gracefully, their eyes fastened on him as if waiting to know his pleasure.

The scholar leaped to his feet, choking back the cry of terror that rose in his throat. He knew, suddenly, without a doubt, what this meant. It was midnight, the moon was at the full, ghosts, evil spirits, witches and goblins would be abroad, filled with power. One of these two creatures standing before him was his wife, known and loved by him all his wedded life—and perhaps not quite fully appreciated, he hastily decided. The other must be a witch, able to change into any form she chose in the twinkling of an eye. But *which was which?* How could he protect his wife and drive this evil double from beside her?

Being a quick thinker as well as a learned one, Kim Su-ik plunged into action. He seized the arm of one of the women with his right hand and before the other could realize what he was about, he had her arm fast in his left hand. They turned mildly reproachful eyes upon him but made no effort to free themselves.

"My dear," said one, "too much study has fevered your brain."

"My dear," said the other, "too much reading of books has affected your mind."

Kim Su-ik looked from one to the other. Not a particle of difference was there to give him a hint as to which was wife and which was witch. He shook them gently. They smiled indulgently as at a child. He shook harder. No resentment, no struggle to get free. He was tempted to relax his grip on the two arms, but he knew he must not for a moment do that, and hung on more firmly than ever.

Minutes went by, then hours, the dull slow moving hours between midnight and cockcrow. The three stood silent, motionless, in the same spot. Kim Su-ik grew weary beyond words. So, too, must his wife be weary, but neither of the two women he held so tightly by the arm said anything or showed by any movement or expression of the face that she was tired, puzzled or angry. His wife would have been tired and puzzled—angry, too, perhaps, but she would not have blustered or scolded. Any other woman would, were she witch or human. But surely his wife would say *something*. What in the world had got into her? Was she bewitched? Or walking in her sleep? Perhaps she was not either one of these two women. He wanted to rush into the other part of the house to see if she was there, thus proving that both of these were witches. But he did nothing, just hung on, grimly, silently.

At long last a cock crowed. Immediately the woman at his left tried to wrench her arm free. The other remained quiet. Kim Su-ik dropped the unresisting one and threw all his strength into a struggle with the other. Like a wild thing the creature fought, biting, snarling, spitting, leaping back and forth. Still the scholar held on to her and would not let go. The arm in his hand shrank and grew hairy. The whole figure dwindled, the eyes grew round and green and blazed with fury.

Another cock crowed and another, and the first gray light of dawn melted the dark shadows out of doors. But Kim Su-ik had no thought or time to notice the coming of day. With a hideous shriek the creature changed before his very eyes into a powerful wildcat. In horror he loosed his hold, and she leaped through the window and was gone.

"I still think you are studying too much," said a quiet, familiar voice behind him, and there stood his wife, pale, trembling a little, but smiling confidently.

"Why didn't you let me know which was which?" demanded Kim Su-ik.

His wife laughed. "I don't know what you are talking about! You behaved very strangely, but then, one never knows what to expect of a scholar. Which was which what?"

"Witch!" said Kim Su-ik.

2. YI CHANG AND THE HAUNTED HOUSE

Yɪ Chang lived in the city of Seoul. He was very poor, very lazy and very friendly. Because he was lazy he did little work, earned less money and rarely had shelter to cover his head. Because he was friendly he found many to wish him well, to talk to him of this and that, and to give him advice as to where he might get him a meal now and then, without too much effort. In short, he was not so poor in heart as he was in bodily possessions. He would have liked very much to have a house of his own, no matter how small and shabby, and was always looking about to see if he could find some tumble-down hut that he could get for little or nothing.

"Now if you were willing to live in a haunted house," said a friend of his one day, "I know of one to be had for the taking."

Yi Chang looked doubtful, then grinned. "Why not?" said he. "I like company. Perhaps a ghost or two would cheer me up on a lonely winter evening. Where is it, this haunted house of which you speak?"

After getting his directions, Yi Chang went to see the place. It stood on a little-traveled road in a section of Seoul called Ink Town at the foot of South Mountain. When he made inquiries about it people shook their heads and clicked their tongues. An old house, rather fine in its day and doubtless still in good repair, they said, but for many years it had been empty. Yes, haunted, without question, but why or by what manner of spirit none knew. Indeed no one had been foolhardy enough to enter the grounds, let alone the house, for as many years back as could be remembered. They strongly advised Yi Chang to have nothing to do with it.

He looked at the place long and questioningly from across the road. Over the weather-stained wall that surrounded it he could see the roof of the house, a tile roof, not one made of grass and thatch like a poor man's dwelling. The corners of it turned up at a proper angle, pagoda fashion, which should make it proof against invading evil spirits. He crossed the road and, after a moment's hesitation, pushed open the gate of the wall and approached the building. A wide clay-floored porch, or matang, extended across the front. Yi Chang skirted it and made his way through a tangle of weeds and garden plants run riot, to the back. There he found the usual kitchen court with a furnace which seemed to be in good condition. There were ample grates and shelves for cooking, and heat evidently had been piped through flues under the floors to keep the house warm in winter.

Yi Chang sighed with satisfaction. Truly, he thought, any man would be more than fortunate to live in such a place. Then he stepped up from the kitchen court into the house itself, there being nothing to prevent him, and looked around. Dust lay thick upon the floor, so thick and so completely untracked that he decided no living feet could have passed over it for years. There were a few bowls and eating utensils lying about, also gray with dust, and spiderwebs hung in the corners of the windows. His courage ebbed a little but he moved slowly across the floor, being as careful as if the stirring up of the dust and breaking of the cobwebs might rouse the dead. Perhaps it might! Ghosts might indeed be sleeping at that moment in the silent rooms and passages beyond. Yi Chang decided he would not explore farther for the present. It would be much pleasanter to have someone with him. Then a thought struck him. Hu and Haw, his two older brothers, lived in a little village not very far from Seoul. They were strong and bold, although a little stupid, perhaps. Why not get them to join him, help him clean up the place—or better, clean it up for him—and stay with him until he had found out a little more about the hauntings? He would tell them just enough to stir their interest and curiosity, not enough to frighten them.

Yi Chang put his thought speedily into action, and soon Hu and Haw, burly country fellows, had joined him and were ready to begin the process of cleaning. Together they went through the whole house. There was nothing unusual to be seen; every room was bare of all furnishings and thick with untracked dust. The paper partitions were whole and the doors slid easily—all except one. In the section of the house customarily reserved for the men of the family, there was one room they could not enter. Curiosity mounted in the three of them as they stood outside that tightly closed door.

At length Hu took a knife from his belt. "Why not thrust through the wall here beside the door? It would be simple enough to make a small peep hole, barely visible."

"Very well," agreed Yi Chang, after a moment's hesitation, for by now he considered himself the owner of the place. "A very small hole will do no harm."

An opening was accordingly made, and Hu, Haw and Yi Chang looked through it in turn and then exchanged puzzled glances.

"A harp with broken strings, a pair of worn shoes, some sticks, an old kettle and a broken sieve," Haw counted off. "Surely no one in his senses would carefully lock up such rubbish!"

"Let us break in the door," suggested Hu, preparing at once to do so.

But Yi Chang held him back. "Not so fast, brother," said he. "Someone has put those things there, someone to whom they mean something. It is best to leave them alone. I shall have plenty of rooms without this one."

So they set about cleaning the house, or rather Hu and Haw cleaned while Yi Chang gave directions and talked in a friendly and affectionate manner. All day they were busy, and only toward sun down did they lay aside their cloths and cleaning sticks. Yi Chang declared he was tired and the other two were willing enough to stop work and go out on the matang. They would rest a bit and eat the food they had brought with them.

But when they had stepped out on the porch, they started back in astonishment. Two large dogs lay sleeping at either end of it. One was tan and the other as black as midnight. Hu and Haw approached the tan dog cautiously while Yi Chang watched. They laid their hands upon the creature, gently at first, and then more roughly. It did not stir.

"Warm?" asked Yi Chang.

Hu nodded.

"I thought maybe they were dead." He ventured a gentle kick at the black dog. No sign of life except the even motion of his sides as he breathed.

The three looked at each other in growing wonder.

"What *are* they?" questioned Hu. "Surely not natural beasts!"

"Where did they come from? And how did they get in? I closed the gate behind us. I don't like it!" Haw said uneasily.

"It *is* strange—very strange," Yi Chang agreed, "but at least they seem harmless. Let them lie."

Hu and Haw rather reluctantly settled themselves on the clay floor of the porch as far from the dogs as possible. It had been a warm day and the cool of the evening was pleasant. After they had eaten they stretched out and were soon asleep.

Yi Chang sat where he could keep an eye on the animals, for, in spite of his confident words, he was uneasy about them. Long after his two brothers had fallen asleep he watched. Nothing happened, however, and at last he too fell into a doze.

He was aroused by the sound of pattering steps on the clay flooring. By the light of a bright moon that was now riding the skies he could see the two dogs, who had left their stations, restlessly pacing back and forth, sniffing the air, then nosing the ground, as if seeking for a scent.

A gong from a distant temple rang the hour. Midnight. Immediately the dogs, facing the moon, began to bay drearily. The sound wakened Hu and Haw who, with stifled screams of alarm, would have made off had not Yi Chang grasped them, one with each hand.

"Idiots!" he hissed as they wrenched themselves free. "Cowards! What are you afraid of? Two dogs baying at the moon?"

Rather shamefaced, the two turned back.

"See, they are paying no attention whatever to us! Let us get into the shadows and watch," Yi Chang suggested.

The three backed into a corner of the porch into which the light of the moon did not penetrate.

Almost at once the howling of the dogs changed to sharp, delighted barks of welcome and they began jumping about, wagging their tails and showing every sign of happy greeting to a loved master. And there on the center of the porch, his slender white hands caressing their heads, stood a strange figure. It was a little old gentleman dressed in ceremonial costume; a long white garment of rich silk, with flowing sleeves, the collar cut according to the careful usage of men of high social standing. On his head was the customary horsehair hat with a narrow crown cut off like a truncated pyramid. The stem of the long curved pipe in his mouth showed white in the moonlight.

How he had got onto the porch without the three seeing him they could not imagine. Perhaps the moon had slipped under a cloud, but it was very clear and bright at that moment and they noticed that neither man nor dogs, standing in the full light of it, cast any shadow.

The old gentleman now entered the house and the dogs returned to their posts at either end of the veranda.

It took not a little urging and reassuring on the part of Yi Chang to persuade his brothers to follow him indoors and see what their curious visitor might be doing. Finally they agreed, keeping Yi Chang well ahead of them and being ready to flee at the slightest hint of danger.

They had no light save that of the moon shining in through windows and doors. Corners and inner passageways were black and threatening. The three tiptoed silently from room to room, pausing often to listen. Not a sound broke the stillness. All doors were open as they had left them after cleaning the place, and the heavy paper partitions separating the rooms gave no hint of light or motion behind them, at least until they reached the locked room.

Hu, Haw and Yi Chang stood motionless, scarcely breathing. It was not a sound exactly but a sense of motion, the barest possible whisper and stir, that issued from that closed and mysterious apartment. Through the paper walls they became aware of a faint luminousness which was not really light but a slight thinning of the heavy dark. The three drew closer together, trembling.

The light from within grew brighter and suddenly chords of music, weird, high, exciting, burst forth—dance music! The shuffling of a pair of shoes could be heard, then laughter and gay voices, the rattling of sticks, the hollow tones of a kettle struck as if it were a drum, and dominating the rhythm the sweet, vibrant chords of a harp.

Yi Chang, full of wonder, left the other two and crept noiselessly to the hole Hu had pierced in the wall beside the sliding bamboo doors. He was just about to put his eye to it when a sword blade was shot through from within—a blue steel blade that glittered with unearthly light. Yi Chang barely avoided it by a sudden jump to one side.

Then the three fled in panic, never minding the clatter they made as they rushed through the house to the clay porch and from that to the gate of the wall and out into the street.

The next morning they consulted together. Hu and Haw were for returning to their home farm without delay. They had had enough, said they, of Seoul in general and of that evil, haunted house in particular. But Yi Chang was not satisfied. Now, in the broad daylight, the house and grounds looked ordinary enough with no sign of anything unusual.

"We spent yesterday there safely," he said to his uneasy brothers. "Why not go through the house once again and see whether those ghostly revelers have left anything interesting behind them?"

Rather unwillingly Hu and Haw agreed. The house, when they had entered it, showed the effects of their cleaning but otherwise was as empty and harmless-looking as could be imagined.

When they reached the locked room Yi Chang very cautiously put his eye to the peep hole. Everything was exactly as it had been before. Harp, sticks, kettle, shoes, sieve, were standing just where they had been and were thick with dust. Yi Chang drew back; the other two looked through into the room, then questioningly at each other.

Hu had an idea. "Look you," said he, speaking in a whisper, as if afraid unseen creatures might be listening. "I have often heard it said that the way to drive off ghosts and evil spirits is to burn the objects that they use."

"Ai!" exclaimed Haw, "the very thing! Let us break through into this haunted room, gather up the articles there and burn them out in the garden."

Yi Chang hesitated but finally nodded a reluctant consent.

It was easy enough to break the heavy paper walls. The three, being uneasy and fearful, worked with speed and soon had the oddly assorted contents of the room piled in the garden with dry leaves and twigs under and over them, ready for a light.

But Yi Chang was worried and unhappy. He watched with a long face and mournful eyes as the fire caught and began to lick the harp. Suddenly he leaped into the blaze and pulled it out. While the other two gaped in amazement he stamped and beat upon the flames, at the same time seizing one object after another and throwing it to safety.

"By the soul of my maternal ancestor," cried Haw, "what are you doing?"

And as Yi Chang made no answer, Hu pulled at his sleeve. "Don't you know we are doing the only thing that will rid your house of ghosts and goblins?"

Yi Chang stopped stamping out the blaze, which was nearly smothered, and brushed the smoke and ashes from his clothing before he answered. "That is just it," he said. "This house is no more mine than *theirs,* whoever they are. And besides, they sound like very gay company. Why should I destroy their simple possessions and so spoil their festivities?"

"I suppose you may even be minded to join them at some ghostly revel!" said Haw sarcastically.

"Until they hang you upside down in a tree or beat you to death or bury you in a deserted tomb! Ghosts and goblins do such things, you know!" Hu snorted in disgust as he spoke.

Yi Chang merely shrugged his shoulders and grinned.

"Very well," said Haw, "we will leave you to your haunted house and ghostly company. Come, Hu, let us return to our peaceful home in the country!"

With that, the two brothers Hu and Haw went off without another word.

As for Yi Chang, he gathered up the broken-stringed harp, the worn shoes, the kettle, the sticks and the sieve and returned them to the room from which they had been taken. With much care he mended the torn wall, even patching up the peep hole so that he would have no further temptation to pry. The next day he settled himself in the haunted house.

Weeks passed, months, a year. Then Hu and Haw, unable

to bear their curiosity any longer, returned to Seoul and be-
took themselves to Ink Town at the foot of South Mountain.
They intended to find out about their brother before telling
him of their arrival and so sought out neighbors secretly to
ask about him.

"Yes, oh yes, the lad Yi Chang is still living in the haunted
house," said one.

"And very happy and prosperous he seems," said another.

"Always ready with a smile or a friendly nod whenever he
sees any of us," said a third. "Friendly—that's what he is.
One cannot help liking him though he must be an odd one,
the way he goes on living over yonder."

"Maybe the house is not haunted any more?" suggested
Hu.

The three neighbors smiled and winked knowingly at each
other. "There is no maybe about it. It is still haunted!" said
the first with authority. But beyond that no one would say
anything.

Hu and Haw hesitated and consulted together and decided
they would investigate further. So, shortly before midnight,
they were again on the road outside their brother's house,
watching, listening and wondering.

The temple gong struck the hour. Immediately they heard
the baying of dogs beyond the wall, then welcoming barks.
Very cautiously they stepped inside the gate. The house was
in total darkness and silence. They waited breathlessly. In a
few moments a light glowed from the house, music sounded,
laughter, and the chattering of voices. The shuffle of dancing
feet kept time to the rhythmic, highly accented music in

which the mellow tones of the harp could be heard. It seemed as if the whole house must be shaken with it. The two, in a panic, rushed for the gate in the wall, only to find themselves face to face with Yi Chang.

"Well, my brothers," said he, "have you come to pay me a visit?"

"N-n-no," stammered Hu, "not exactly."

"We—we—just happened to be passing," added Haw, edging closer to the gate.

"And you must leave so soon?" Yi Chang smiled and then laughed. "I thought I might persuade you to join me and my companions in our festivity tonight."

"Your companions?" Hu repeated in awe. "Then you—you—have really made friends with them? You are not afraid?"

"No, not at all," said Yi Chang. "Why should one be afraid of friends?"

"But—who *are* they?" whispered Haw. "*What* are they?"

Yi Chang shrugged his shoulders and answered indifferently. "I do not really know, but does it matter? They are friends. Come! I will make you acquainted with them!"

But Hu and Haw would not be persuaded. Another look at the house with its one glowing window and its strange, unearthly music growing wilder every moment was enough for them. They bade Yi Chang farewell and hurried away. Behind them they heard their brother's steps on the matang floor, the excited, happy barking of two dogs greeting him, and many thin, faint voices shouting welcome.

After they had walked for a long time in silence through

the deserted streets of Seoul, Hu said, "He is a very friendly person, our brother Yi Chang."

"Yes," agreed Haw thoughtfully. "And it is a good thing to be friendly; one can see that—friendly with everybody."

"Even with ghosts?" Hu's voice sounded a little doubtful but Haw spoke with conviction.

"Even with ghosts!"

3. TIGER WOMAN

Nᴵᴹ Sᴀɴ had a large family of boys and girls, but no wife. Since her death they had all lived with his mother, a gentle old lady who spoiled the children and could never say no to their desires. They had brass-studded chests filled with strings of money, each coin with a hole in its center so that a large number could be strung on a single cord. All Korean households kept their money in strings, and Nim San was fortunate in the length and number that he had stored away. He was a rich man. But there comes an end to all good material possessions if they are not replenished, and there came a time when the last string had been taken out of the last chest and there soon would not be a single coin left.

Nim San was dismayed, but not the children. They had always had everything they wanted and had never stopped to consider how or where their father had got it.

"Please, Honorable Parent," said one of the boys, "I shall need a new padded coat for the winter. Mine is much too short in the sleeves."

"We shall all need new coats for the New Year festival," cried the other boys.

"And new straw sandles, and wooden-soled boots for the rainy season—and soft shoes, too, with the toes turning up."

"And we need another kang-jar for kimchee—there are so many of us," the grandmother put in.

"And lots and lots of silk string and colored paper for our new kites," said the littlest boy.

"Honorable Father," one of the girls managed to put her word in. "I am old enough for a jeweled comb and all of us need new ribbons." A chorus of "ye', ye' " came from all the little girls who had gathered around him. "We want— We want—"

"There are sweetmeats in Seoul better than our home-made ones—"

"Will you buy us—"

"Father, we need—"

Nim San threw up his hands in despair. "But, my children, there is no more money left!"

Silence followed for a few moments, then the chatter broke out again. "But, Honorable Father, we must have—" And so it went, more demanding than ever. Apparently nobody, not even Grandmother, could understand that without money there could be no more buying. Nim San tried to explain but at last gave it up and fled from the house, unable to bear the situation longer.

Not far from his home the mountains began. Their green wooded sides were showing patches of gold and scarlet, russet and purple, for the autumn frosts were already tingling in the air, but Nim San had no eyes for the beauty around him. His heart was so heavy that he thought he might better die.

He climbed up and up, scarcely noticing where he was going, and when at last he roused himself from his sad thoughts and looked around, he realized that he was in a part of the country quite strange to him. He was not exactly lost, for the trail he had absent-mindedly followed was definite and wound on around the side of the hill and undoubtedly would lead him somewhere. Near him he noticed a small grass-roofed hut close to the steep mountain, and as he felt suddenly very weary, he walked over to it, pushed the bamboo door open and stepped inside. A light snow had begun to fall and he felt chilled to the very marrow of his bones.

There being, of course, no heat inside the hut, it seemed damp and colder than outside, so he left the door open, sitting on the floor beside the high sill.

Before long he was astonished to see, coming up the trail toward him, a very beautiful sedan chair richly fitted out with silken hangings and borne by four runners in handsome livery. They came close to the hut and then paused, the bearers breathing heavily after their hard climb. Behind them at some distance an elderly woman in the customary dress of a servant followed, moving slowly and with difficulty, almost at the end of her strength.

The curtains of the chair parted and a woman looked out. Upon seeing Nim San she withdrew again in confusion, for it is not proper for a woman to be seen by any strange man, much less to converse with him. But after a moment she looked out again, motioned her bearers to set down the chair and stepped out. She paid no attention to Nim San but ran back to the old woman, put a supporting arm about her and led her to the hut. Nim San, bowing courteously, moved aside and helped settle the exhausted servant on the floor. Impulsively he took his own padded coat off and laid it over her, for she was shivering in spite of her layers of cotton clothing.

Then Nim San and the lady from the sedan chair looked at each other. Never had he seen so beautiful or so unusual a face; young, with skin like palely tinted ivory, red lips and delicate pointed chin, hair as black as midnight, and thin black eyebrows. From under these her narrow slanted eyes stared out at him—green like those of a cat. Noticing his astonishment, the lady smiled faintly, and Nim San was covered with confusion at his own rudeness.

"Honorable Lady," said he, bowing very low, "I ask a thousand pardons. I—I—is there not something I can do for you or for your woman? The snow is falling more heavily now and already the evening chill has sharpened the air—" He paused, scarcely knowing how to meet the unblinking keenness of those green eyes.

"Thank you, good Sir " The lady's voice was silken soft, unlike any he had ever heard. "You have already shown a remarkably unselfish kindness in placing your own coat over my old nurse, but now you must put it on again before you are chilled through."

She clapped her hands and the bearers of the sedan came forward. Following her commands, they carried the old woman to the chair, laid her within it, and handed Nim San his coat again.

"And now," continued the lady, "I bid you follow after me. My house lies not many miles distant, in the heart of a hidden valley. There you will be welcome as my guest and can pass the night in warmth and comfort, and continue your journey in the morning." She climbed again into the sedan chair and drew the curtains. The runners picked up the poles and started at a jog trot, taking the trail farther into the mountains.

Nim San followed them. He had some difficulty in keeping their pace and soon fell behind, but in time he rounded a beetling bluff and came upon a narrow road leading straight down into a deep valley.

The snow had ceased falling and the air was tangy with the scent of evergreens. The sun came out and it seemed warmer as he descended. Then the pines and hemlocks gave place to trees whose flaming scarlet and gold vied with the sunset splendor of the western sky.

A large and beautiful palace stood directly in front of him, almost as fine and extensive as the emperor's own. Servants met him and took him to the men's apartment, where he bathed and put on the rich white silk apparel which they laid out for him. Then on a gold and lacquer tray his dinner was brought to him, served in shining brass bowls—rice and beans, fowl and kimchee and many special delicacies, all of the best and tastiest. He sat on his heels on the floor in front of the tray and, finding himself very hungry, made a good meal of it.

After the empty bowls and the spoons and chopsticks had been removed and he had washed his fingers in scented water, he was taken to the inner court, where he found the lady waiting to receive him. The old slave woman had evidently recovered for she sat crouched in a corner of the room, as motionless as a statue.

They had a pleasant evening together. The lady was gracious and friendly. She soon put him at his ease and he found himself telling of his motherless children, their continual but entirely understandable demands and his despair at being now unable to supply them.

The lady bade him lay aside his cares. "I live in this big house alone but for my old nurse and the other servants," she said. "There is no end to my wealth and my possessions, and most gladly will I give you all that you desire. Tomorrow morning my servants will load a donkey for you with presents for your honorable mother and for the children, and strings of money for you to use as you have need. Only be my friend and come again to my palace when the winter evenings are long and cold. We will play at changki (chess) together and while away the long hours sitting here upon the warm floor. And always when you come I will supply all your needs for your home and family."

Nim San could do nothing but bow over and over again, murmuring his thanks while tears of relief and gratitude ran down his cheeks.

The next morning he found a donkey laden with the gifts from the lady standing in the courtyard. Servants stood about ready to serve him but he saw no sign of their mistress and at last left his good-byes and repeated thanks with the head man who promised to deliver them, and started on the long journey home.

The surprise and delight of his old mother and still more of his children can well be imagined and for a long time there were no demands from them. Nim San lived happily enough in the midst of his contented family, with money to spare and all their needs and desires satisfied. He thought often of the strange beautiful lady with the green eyes and her rich palace on the other side of the mountains and at length decided to visit her again as he had agreed to do.

He had no trouble in finding his way though it was a long and difficult climb and bitter cold now that winter had set in. The lady seemed more lovely and charming than ever, and after that, all through the winter, he visited her again and yet again. Often she loaded him with gifts, but not always. Sometimes they would just spend a contented evening together playing chess or talking. He would sleep on a thick mat on the warm comfortable floor in the men's apartment and then go home the next morning without seeing her again and with no gifts or messages from her. He began to prefer not to be always indebted to her, for he realized that he loved her and wanted to make her his wife. The rich gifts he was constantly receiving from her, while he gave her nothing in return, made things awkward. Indeed the whole situation was awkward. There seemed to be no one who could act as a go-between for her, as is customary in all Korean marriages. Always the old nurse sat on her heels, motionless as a stone image, in the room with them, but there appeared to be no relative or proper person to whom his mother could go and discuss marriage for him.

Nim San was thinking about these things one day in early spring as he climbed the steep trail over the mountain. Suddenly he saw a strange white cloud rolling down upon him. It seemed like a huge soft ball so distinct and round that he expected to feel the impact of it as it fell upon him. He did not, however. It quietly surrounded him, shutting out instantly all sight of the valley beneath him and the tops of the hills above him and even the newly budding trees and bushes all around him. Mist, gray, thick, damp, cold, closed him in so completely that he stopped where he was, not daring to take a step forward or back.

Suddenly from somewhere above his head he heard a harsh

voice saying, "Get down upon the ground, Nim San. Make reverent obeisance to the soul of your ancestor."

Nim San, trembling with terror, fell upon his knees, covering his eyes with his hands. "What would you, Great and Honorable Sir?" he said, touching his head to the earth nine times.

"I have come from the world beyond the farthest mountains to warn you," the voice continued. "Listen carefully to what I say and obey me."

There was a long moment of silence. Nim San, though still shaking with fear and astonishment, dropped his hands and looked about him. He could see nothing but the blank gray wall of mist. "Speak further, Honorable Ancestor," said he tremblingly. "Your humble and dutiful descendant is listening."

"The woman you are bent upon visiting"—the voice was harsher than ever—"is no ordinary mortal, but a tiger. Did you not note the green eyes of her? Tiger-woman she is in very truth, permitted only for certain hours to take upon herself the form of a human."

Nim San gasped and then groaned. He had not realized the strength of his love for the lady but now the thought of losing her, of her being other than she seemed, cut his heart deeply and miserably.

"Waste no time in foolish sorrow," the voice went on in a cold, pitiless tone. "Go at once to the palace as you intended. Do not wait for the servants to admit you but thrust open the bamboo door of the inner court *without knocking*. Then you will see the lady of your love in her true and terrible state.

What is more important, if you catch her in the act of changing herself into human form she will have to continue a beast, a fierce and hated tiger, forever."

With that the mist folded back like a blanket, rolled down the mountainside and disappeared. The sun shone again over the hill tops for a few moments, then dropped behind them, for the late afternoon was wearing on. The trail showed clearly with the rough underbrush crowding it, and the valley in the distance grew soft in the lovely shades of the early spring twilight.

For a few moments Nim San was too shocked and bewildered to move. Then he got to his feet and, without allowing himself time to think, hurried on. He reached the palace just as the half light was darkening into night, rushed through the outer court to the bamboo door of the women's apartment. He was about to thrust it open without knocking, as he had been bidden to do, when something stayed his hand. Though the green-eyed lady might indeed be a terrible tiger, able by some magic art to appear human and deceive him, he could not take a mean advantage over her. Many a time her strange eyes had looked into his with kindness, friendliness and even love. She had been good to him and to his children. He could not find it in his heart thus to betray her.

His hand dropped and he was about to turn away from the bamboo door when it slowly opened. The old nurse stood there and silently motioned him to come in. Then she left him and for some time he remained alone, standing with his hands in his sleeves, his head bowed, wondering.

She entered again, noiselessly. Nim San did not hear or

see her come. But suddenly he found the lady with her standing in front of him, more beautiful and gracious than ever,
tall, slim, in rich silken garments white as snow. Fearfully
he looked into her face and cried out in his astonishment. Her
eyes were no longer green but black and sparkling with joy
and affection and—yes—amusement!

"Do not look so dumfounded, dear friend," said she,
laughing. "All is as it should be! Come!" She led the way into
the inner court and bade him sit beside her on the warm floor.

"You have this day saved me from a thousand years of
grief and torment," she said. "In the spirit world I was condemned, for a sin I had committed, to take the form of a tiger
for many generations. But every once in so often, for certain
hours and certain days, it was permitted me to change into
human form. If during my time as a woman I could win the
love of a good man who, in spite of knowing my other state,
would marry me, then I was to be allowed to stay human.
There was one condition, however: neither he nor anyone
must ever see me in the act of changing from tiger to woman
or woman to tiger. If any mortal eyes should behold that
great, mysterious act of magic, which none but the spirits that
dwell beyond the farthest mountains know about or understand, then I would be condemned to keep my tiger shape
unchanged for a thousand years, perhaps forever."

"So the soul of my ancestor spoke the truth," Nim San murmured, "but not the whole truth, and I would rather have you
as my wife, whatever shape or form you held in some past
life, than any woman in this world or that Other."

The lady's black almond eyes grew soft and tears welled

up in them. "You see," she said, brushing away the bright drops, "this proves I am altogether human for neither beasts nor spirits, good or bad, can shed tears as humans do."

"But why should the soul of my ancestor counsel me to a deed of discourtesy and unkindness that would result only in sorrow to both of us?" Nim San was still puzzled.

"That was not the soul of your ancestor!" declared the lady. "It was an evil spirit that has long pursued me to destroy me, body and soul, forever! But now he can have no further power over me."

"Why is that?" asked Nim San, wondering.

"Because love is stronger than any evil," said the lady.

Now the rest of the story is easily guessed. Nim San married the lovely lady and took his children and his mother to the beautiful palace on the other side of the mountain. There they lived in great happiness together for the rest of their days.

4. THE STATUE THAT SNEEZED

EVERYONE said Sim Kiong was a lazy worthless fellow. In summer he did nothing from morning till night but sit on his veranda smoking a clay pipe so long he could not light it himself but had to call his young son to light it for him. And all through the cold winter days he dozed on the warm floor in the portion of his house reserved for the men and boys of the family.

He had a wife and four children. The wife did nothing

41

but nag and scold him, with good reason, it must be admitted, because day by day they had less to eat, fewer clothes to cover them, and a surer expectation of having to leave their home and beg on the streets to get a living. But the children loved their father. Sometimes he would play games with them—if they were not too lively. Often he would go fishing with his son, and many a time when his boy and his three little girls were chattering together in the inner court of the house, he would call them to him and, between puffs on his long pipe, tell them stories marvelous to hear—and quite impossible to believe. The children did not worry because their father was a poor provider, so long as he was such an excellent teller of tales.

One summer day Sim Kiong got more than an earful from his wife, who finally bade him begone out of her sight until he could find something to mend their fortune or at least fill their stomachs.

Sim shrugged his shoulders, smiled wryly and apologetically and, without a word in self-defense, turned and walked through the gate of the wall that surrounded his house. The road before him ran in one direction into Seoul, in the other it led to the distant mountains. One could probably find work in the city, but in the hills, whither Sim had never yet gone, one might find treasure, adventure or good luck of some kind. He might come upon a precious stone or perhaps a nugget of gold; or, at the very least, he might dig up a root of ginseng, that magic weed which Koreans powder and use as medicine for all diseases. Sim turned his back on Seoul and walked steadily in the other direction.

After many hours of hot weary tramping he found himself in a green valley surrounded by wooded hills. A rough overgrown trail had replaced the road, and it straggled up and over a ridge, then down into a clearing in which he could see the ruins of an ancient shrine. There, pressed upon by trees and overgrown with vines and bushes, stood a gigantic stone statue of Buddha. Sim, looking up at its face, judged that the nose must be at least four feet long, the mouth with its full lips four feet wide, and its eyes under beetling granite brows of like proportions. A huge slab of rock served as a hat, and down over the whole figure poured wild grapevines and ivy. Out of a deep crack in the hat of the statue a pear tree was growing, and at the end of one of its branches hung a large, luscious-looking pear.

Sim Kiong laughed aloud. "There," said he to himself, "is my find, my treasure! I will pluck that pear and carry it back to my children. One fifth will be enough for a meal for each child and for my wife. Ai-goo! it is too bad but I shall have to go hungry!"

With that he set foot in the tough vines and by hard climbing and scrambling soon got himself up to the lips of the stone figure, directly under its nose. There, breathing heavily, he paused and considered his next move. From the mouth to the forehead there was nothing to cling to except the nose, which was far too wide and too slippery to get a grip on. The pear hung out from the tree not far from his reach, but by no amount of straining or struggling could he touch it. If he could climb up that smooth granite nose to the jagged crack in the rock hat out of which the tree grew, he might be able to reach it or, if not, he could shake the tree until the fruit loosened and fell down.

There was no possible means, however, by which he could climb that nose. He was about to give up when an idea occurred to him. Looking into the nose, he saw that light came in through a break in the bridge of it and showed the inner surface to be rough and nobbly. To climb up inside would be an easy matter. Then he could wriggle through the hole in the bridge and come out almost at the foot of the pear tree.

No sooner thought than put into action. Sim Kiong climbed up into the giant stone nose. He had almost reached the top when, whee! ka-choo-oo! a loud explosion nearly deafened him and a wind with the strength of a hurricane blew him out of the nose and landed him on the ground yards away from the statue. When he could get his breath he looked around. Close beside him lay the pear, also blown down. He grasped it quickly before anything else could happen to him. Then he looked back at the great stone Buddha. A gentle pink suffused the giant face, the eyes held each a large round drop of moisture and the nose was definitely twitching!

Again, a-ka-choo! a-ka-choo! A blast of sound, a fierce gale of wind, and Sim, still tightly grasping the pear, was swept over the treetops, out of the valley, and dumped down on the very road he had traveled from home not so many hours before.

He picked himself up, dusted himself off and, finding he was none the worse for his adventure, moved along at a smart pace. Soon he had reached the gate in his own wall, had flung it open and was mounting the veranda.

"Come, children, come, wife of my heart, see what I have brought you!" he shouted.

Wondering, they came hurrying out to greet him. He called for a knife and with great skill cut the huge pear into five equal parts. "There," he said, giving a share to his wife, to his son and to his three little girls. "Now, tell me, have you ever eaten anything like that before?"

They never had, and what is more, after each had eaten a fifth of the pear and declared himself as satisfied as with a large dinner, behold! the core, which Sim was idly swinging in his hand, took upon itself substance, grew round and full, and there was the whole and perfect fruit again, without a blemish! So he had his share of it also.

Then Sim Kiong told his adventure to the astonished family, enlarging a little perhaps on his difficulties and the behavior of the stone Buddha—just enough to make a dramatic story out of it.

When it was finished there was a long moment of silence, then his son said, "Honorable Father, never before have you told such a wonderful tale. And here is the proof of the wonder, a magic fruit which replenishes itself. Father, let us go, you and I, to the city of Seoul; let us get ourselves a booth in the market place. Then, when the crowds gather, you can tell this story, and others you have told us, and you can show the pear and eat a bit of it and—"

Sim Kiong laughed aloud, caught his boy by his long hair and playfully swung him around into his arms.

"Son," said he, "truly you are destined to become a mighty pak-sa, a scholar of scholars, and your father is not too proud to profit by your suggestion. We will indeed tell stories in the market place, at least I will, and at the most exciting spot, as is customary, I will pause and you will hand around a bowl and collect strings of money!"

The boy nodded vigorously. "We could even let someone eat a piece of the pear—for a price—and watch it grow itself again."

"We will call our story 'The Pear of Wonder,'" said the father musingly.

"Or 'The Statue That Sneezed,'" suggested the son.

5. A BOY AND A BEGGAR

IN THE days of King Chung-jong, some four hundred years
ago, there lived in the city of Seoul a beggar, a magician,
and a young student named Wun-yoo. Of course there were
many beggars in the city then, as now; there were also many
boys studying at the schools and in the palace; and there
were many magicians, more than at any time since. But it
chanced that the lives of these three crossed, and the result
was a strange and marvelous adventure for Wun-yoo.

He was a clever lad and knew his books. Even at the age of

twelve years he was well read in the Chinese classics and could write poetry with a brush as delicate and lovely as the thoughts he inscribed with it. His father, who was proud of him though he never said so, allowed more of his poems to be pinned upon the walls of his home than he did those of any of his brothers or cousins, and now had sent him, in spite of his youth, to live in Seoul and attend the classes in a school for the sons of yangbans (noblemen).

Wun-yoo was on his way to school one day when he met the magician Chon U-chi and the beggar. Chon U-chi was astride a donkey so small that his feet barely escaped the ground. One servant walked at the donkey's head to guide it, and another walked behind it, carrying scrolls and books for his master. Such sights were not uncommon on the streets of Seoul, but what followed was most uncommon indeed. There came slowly along from the other direction a very ragged and dirty-looking beggar. Chon U-chi took one keen look at his face and immediately dismounted from the donkey. There in the mud and filth of the open street, he got down on his knees and kow-towed nine times before him.

Wun-yoo was astonished. Magicians were proud and lordly folk and Chon U-chi had the reputation of being more haughty than any of them.

The beggar inclined his head in recognition of the tribute paid him, motioned Chon to rise, bowed again with solemn dignity and passed on.

Wun-yoo still stood with his mouth wide open and his eyes fairly popping out of his head. The great Chon U-chi looked at him and laughed.

"Small wonder you are gaping with surprise, my son," said he. "It is evident from your books and dress that you are a student. But mark my words, you will never be truly wise, no matter how much you know, if you do not learn to look through appearances to the truth underneath them."

"I scarce know what you mean," said Wun-yoo, bowing politely with his hands in the sleeves of his padded jacket. "Would it please your honorable nobility to explain?"

"Yon beggar," continued the magician, indicating the figure disappearing down the street, "whom you saw covered with rags and dirt, with his hair down his back like an unmarried schoolboy, is Chang To-ryong, one of the three greatest and most powerful spirit-men in the whole of Chosen, or Korea, as moderns prefer to call it."

"Then why—" began Wun-yoo, more puzzled than ever. But Chon U-chi cut him short.

"Why is a stupid question. Find him again, see him, look at him—*him,* not his wretched outside." He mounted his donkey and motioned the two waiting servants to move on. He took a few grains of rice from the pocket in his embroidered belt and put them in his mouth. Then he blew them out again in the form of delicate blue butterflies which circled around his head in a fluttering cloud of loveliness.

Wun-yoo remained staring, rooted to the spot, until the magician turned into a side street and was gone.

After that he sought through all the alleys and slums of Seoul, wherever beggars gathered, to find Chang and have another and a better look at him. Before very long he found him. This time Wun-yoo looked keenly into his face, and

thereafter never thought of the man as mean or wretched,
even though he was poor and begged. Often Wun-yoo went
hungry, to fill the man's begging bowl with food that he had
saved from his own meals.

Chang To-ryong had a wonderful face. His eyes were deep
and wise, yet had a merry twinkle in them. His lips seemed
always ready to smile, but never in scorn, rather in friendliness and understanding. The whole look of him was so keen
and kind and knowledgeable it drew the heart of Wun-yoo
right out of him and made him desire the man's friendship,
beggar though he was, more than anything else in the world.
Yet he hesitated to speak to him or approach him. He, Wun-
yoo, was the son of a yangban, a noble magistrate. What
would his father or his schoolmates say if they should see him
talking to a ragged, miserable beggar? So he held himself
aloof, merely dropping good food into Chang's begging bowl
and always smiling, just a little, and shyly, when he passed
him on the street.

Then winter came with raw winds, snow, sleet and bitter
cold. Wun-yoo was unhappy about Chang. As he tossed
about on his sleeping mat on the warm floor at night, he
kept imagining the bleak, ice-cold streets and wretched
broken-down huts where the beggars of Seoul would be huddled together, trying to keep themselves from freezing. At
last he could stand it no longer. Rising from his mat one cold
stormy night, he put on his padded coat and heavy baggy
trousers and went out to look for Chang To-ryong.

He found him at length in a mean, tumbled-down, wind-
blown hovel at the edge of the city. Chang was alone, and to

the boy's suggestion that he come to his student lodging place and take his bed, he said nothing, merely nodding his head in agreement.

The cold rain had turned to sleet and stung their faces as, with heads bent against it, they hurried along. Wun-yoo felt frozen to the very marrow of his bones when they had got back to his dwelling. Chang's hair and face glistened with wet as they stepped into the dimly lighted room where the sleeping mats were spread. His hands looked blue with cold and his wet garments clung soddenly to him. The boy had no clothes of his own that were large enough for the man, but he shamelessly offered some that belonged to a bigger boy, a fellow student, absent at the time. He would explain, make his friend understand, he thought to himself hastily. There was something about Chang's face, a look, a kind of radiance, which made one want to give him everything one had or could lay one's hands on.

Several times during that winter Wun-yoo brought Chang into his own room, housed him, fed him, took care of him. Always the beggar accepted what was done for him and gave in return that strange, warming look of gratitude, friendliness and understanding. He said very little, yet Wun-yoo felt more than repaid—and loved him.

Then at last spring came, the sun shone down warmly on the streets of Seoul and there was less reason for Wun-yoo to worry about his friend the beggar. He was very busy. Examinations had been proclaimed and, like all students, his mind became entirely occupied with his reading and his verse making. He forgot all about Chang To-ryong. He made a mark

for himself in his work, was highly commended and promised a place among the king's officials, like his father, when he
grew older.

Home seemed very good to him when he went back. The
family lived comfortably enough in a village not far from
the city, and he settled again into his accustomed life as if
he had never left it. The summer days hurried by, and it was
not until he was in Seoul again that the young student be-
thought him of his strange acquaintance.

Again he looked for Chang To-ryong among all the beggars who swarmed the streets, went through the slums and
alleys where the poorest were gathered, but nowhere did he
catch sight of the man or hear any rumor of his where-
abouts.

Then, at last, passing near the Water Gate, Wun-yoo saw
him—and for the last time, he believed. A plain bare
stretcher was being borne through the gate by two ragged
bearers, and on the stretcher, uncovered except for the tattered and dirty clothes he had always worn, lay Chang To-
ryong. The boy ran up, stopped the bearers and gazed long
and tearfully at the dead, shrunken face.

"Ai-goo! Ai-goo!" He sighed. "Perhaps he would not have
died thus if I had not neglected and forgotten him!" He
turned away, very sorrowful, and was surprised to see the
magician Chon U-chi behind him.

"We meet again," said he briefly. "I see you have learned
to see truly—but not completely." With that he reached for
some rice grains in the pocket of his sash, sucked them
thoughtfully for a moment, then blew them out again. With

his head in a cloud of delicate blue butterflies he walked away.

Some twenty years from that day, when Wun-yoo had grown to be a portly gentleman, a magistrate, the head of his house and the father of a fine family of boys and girls, he set out upon a journey across the Ever White mountains. It was a matter of business and his head was full of figures and calculations so that he scarcely noticed the road over which his jogging little donkey bore him. It was a steep and narrow way, climbing up and up. Vast and beautiful views of the valleys and lower hills opened up before him and changed with every turn he made, but Wun-yoo kept his head bent, busy with his own thoughts, and gave no heed to the majestic splendor all around him.

Suddenly his small beast stopped so abruptly he almost fell forward over its head. He looked up and was astonished to find that the road faced directly into the side of the mountain. There was not so much as a footpath to right or left. Sheer precipices fell away on either side and a bare unbroken slab of rock rose in front of him with mountain crags above as high as he could see. There was nothing he could do but wheel his donkey around in a space scarcely bigger than a coin, and retrace his steps until he could find another road. Undoubtedly he had missed some turning. The donkey, however, thought differently about the matter. Either he was afraid because of the sheer drops on both sides of the narrow road, or he had taken it into his stubborn head to go forward or not move at all. He braced his four stout little legs stiffly and brayed. Wun-yoo knew from experience that a whip only made the donkey more stubborn, so he tried persuasion, but to no avail. He was about to dismount and pull the animal around when, with a grating, roaring sound, the rock face of the mountain in front of him swung open and he saw before him a dark narrow passageway with a square of light at the other end. The donkey did not pause to wonder but trotted right in. The huge rock door rumbled and closed behind them, and there was nothing to do but go on.

The tunnel was not long and opened out into an unbelievably wild and beautiful country. Mountain peaks towered over a green valley in which were small scattered lakes, crystal clear and shining. Waterfalls tumbled chattering across the narrow path over which Wun-yoo rode, and the very pebbles on the ground beneath the donkey's feet shone and glowed with color like so many gems. There was something about the air that caught the heart and lifted it. Never had Wun-yoo felt so happy. He wanted to shout and laugh for sheer joy. He longed for someone to rejoice with him. He slapped the reins on his donkey's back and began to sing a lively air that he used to know as a boy and had not thought of for many years. As he sang the memory of his childhood came back to him and he seemed to see himself playing in the outer court of his home with his brothers and sisters. He heard again in his mind their laughter and shouting as they bounced on the seesaw or chased each other in hide-and-seek. Then clearly and strongly came the pictured memory of himself, twelve years old, standing at a crossroads in Seoul. Again he seemed to see the forlorn and ragged beggar

approaching him and Chon U-chi, the proud magician, bowing in the dust.

The little donkey stumbled and brayed. Wun-yoo raised
his eyes and saw coming toward him on the narrow mountain road a man astride a pure white horse, like a bride-
groom, with servants running before and behind him. As he
drew nearer, Wun-yoo saw that he was clothed in silk of
the softest and loveliest green.

The stranger halted in front of him, dismounted, and with
a courteous bow said, "My friend, you are expected. My
palace awaits your honorable presence. I pray you, come."

There was something about the voice vaguely familiar to
Wun-yoo, and yet it was unlike any voice he had ever heard.
It seemed to mingle with the sound of the mountain stream
slipping down over a nearby precipice, and then again it
melted into the wind so that he wondered whether he had
really heard it at all or only imagined it. There was no doubt-
ing the reality of the stranger, however, and he and his train
of servants had wheeled themselves around and were already
descending the road, evidently expecting Wun-yoo to follow.

He did so, marveling more and more at the strangeness of
the mountain world into which he had come. Snow-capped
peaks broke the line of the far horizon, thin mists, mauve
colored, lay in the valleys, broken now and then by the rays
of the sun into filmy veils of opalescent beauty. The green
ravines, the waterfalls close at hand, and the mirror-clear
lakes in the near distance, were not in themselves different
from what one would expect in a mountainous country.

But there was something more, a sense of otherness, a feeling that nothing was quite real to the touch, to the senses, and yet more true and lasting and beautiful than human life itself. Wun-yoo rode thoughtfully and wonderingly after his guide, scarcely daring to breathe lest the spell be broken and he find himself only dreaming. Happiness flooded his heart, too great for words.

After riding several miles they came in sight of a palace shining in the brightness of the westering sun. It was set upon a hill by itself with only the forests and the towering mountains around it. The man and his servants turned into the road that led to it and Wun-yoo on his little donkey trotted after them.

The palace was built of jade with windows of clear crystal. Once inside the tall bamboo gate in the wall that surrounded it, Wun-yoo felt a little less strange and dumfounded. Children ran about in the outer court, and they smiled at him in friendly fashion. Servants took his donkey. He removed his shoes and left them at the door and followed the man in green to the guest quarters. There his guide laid a friendly hand on his arm, and Wun-yoo looked into his face, keenly, searchingly. Then he knew!

"Chang To-ryong!" he cried joyfully. "Is it you indeed?"

The other nodded. "I have waited long for you to come this way," said he. "You who saw through the wretched outer man to the true one beneath it! You were kind and good to me, my friend, in my exile, and now you must be my guest in this my happier state."

"Exile?" questioned Wun-yoo.

Chang smiled ruefully. "Ah yes, in punishment for a grave fault I was exiled from the spirit world and doomed to live as a beggar in poverty and dire need for a hundred years. Such was my condition when you knew me."

"But—but—" interrupted Wun-yoo, "I saw you with my own eyes lying dead on a stretcher near the Water Gate of Seoul many years ago."

"Not dead, my friend, only journeying home."

Words could not be found to tell all the wonder and beauty and strangeness of Wun-yoo's visit to that Other World. He could never quite remember himself just how long he remained in the company of his friend. He could never describe the sumptuous meals or the music played by unseen hands, or the men, women and children whom he saw moving about that radiant palace. Very beautiful they were, more so than the fairest of mortals, and their faces shone with happiness and their voices rang like silver bells sweetly tuned. Always, all around him lay the beauty of the mountains, the deep blue sky, the air that brought a song to his lips. Never had he known such joy, such a feeling of power and exhilaration! But for him it could not last long. The human body is not able to bear that which is natural to the spirit. So, in time, Chang To-ryong led his friend outside the palace, bade him an affectionate farewell and left him.

What happened then Wun-yoo never quite knew. A mist enveloped him and a heavy sleep closed his eyelids, but only for a moment. When he opened them again he found himself on the other side of the mountains, jogging along on his small donkey. Ahead of him was the city he had set out for

when he left home, and very soon his mind was again completely occupied with figures and calculations.

Only one little adventure crossed his path after his business had been attended to and he was on his way back to his
family. Just inside the Water Gate of Seoul he came upon
Chon U-chi, the magician. The man looked at him with his
keen, much-seeing eyes, then smiled and nodded his head
approvingly. He said nothing but took from the pocket of his
gold-embroidered belt a small handful of rice which he put
in his mouth. Then immediately he blew the grains out again
and they became a cloud of delicate blue butterflies.

Wun-yoo smiled indulgently and passed on. What were
magic butterflies to a man who had been the guest of a great
spirit in that Other World? He would tell that part of his
story to his children, however, the little ones. They would
love to hear about the blue butterflies. Only to those who
could understand would he tell his most wonderful experience, how he had looked once and seen a wretched beggar,
had looked a second time more deeply and had begun to see,
beneath the ugly tattered rags, a citizen of the spirit world.

6. THE REVENGE OF THE SERPENT

THERE was once a young woodcutter whose name was Kil Tong. He was a kindly soul always ready to lend a helping hand to man or beast in need of it.

Now it happened one day while he was at work in the woods that he heard a great outcry and commotion, a fluttering and a squawking in the underbrush not far from where he stood. Two pheasants, a male and a female, were making a great to-do, and for good reason as he soon discovered, for a large green snake lay coiled a few feet from their nest and was threatening their young. Kil Tong made short work of the serpent, killing it with one swift, carefully aimed blow of a thick stick. Then he went back to his woodcutting and the pheasants settled quietly to their domestic affairs. The boy soon forgot the whole matter.

Many years later he had occasion to travel through these same woods, which had become, in the meantime, denser and harder to penetrate. The trail was badly marked and after some time he realized that he was lost. Several hours of plunging about in the thick underbrush seemed only to carry him deeper into the forest and bewilder him the more.

"Ai-goo!" said he. "Here are the shadows of evening falling upon me and I know not how to go either forward or back!"

The thought of tigers that undoubtedly ranged the forest at night made him tremble with fear, and as the woods grew darker he imagined green eyes staring hungrily out at him from every black thicket.

"If I could but find a deserted hut to shelter me through the night!" he muttered to himself, and at that very moment he caught sight of a lighted lantern swaying among the branches of the trees not many yards beyond him. He hastened toward it as best he could through the tangle of roots and bushes and at last came out into a small clearing. The lantern stood before the door of a low hut, and toward this Kil Tong made his way, much relieved in mind. Undoubtedly the owner would allow him to spend the night in its shelter and be able to direct him back to the right trail in the morning.

He rapped on the door, which was immediately opened. In the doorway, framed by a light coming from within, her face palely visible in the dim glow, stood a young and beautiful woman. Never had Kil Tong looked at so fair a face, such black almond-shaped eyes, such clear ivory skin or so lovely a figure. And yet—and yet—his heart went cold within him and, for no reason at all, he had a sudden desire to run back into the depths of the forest. Even the terror of tigers was, for the moment, as nothing to his sudden sense of immediate danger.

Before he could speak the young maid smiled and, putting forth a graceful arm, drew him into the hut and closed the door.

Kil Tong bowed respectfully and asked after the master of the house. Once inside, his queer sense of fear left him as suddenly as it had come.

"The master will be back presently," said the girl in a silken voice. "Meanwhile I have set food upon a little table and invite you to eat." She motioned to the customary low table set with brass bowls, spoons and chopsticks.

A faint aroma of hot rice and kimchee rose invitingly to his nostrils. He looked again questioningly at the lady, then, obeying her motion, knelt upon the floor and began to eat hungrily.

"You see, you were expected." The girl's voice at his back sounded so like a hissing whisper that Kil Tong started nervously.

The food was good, wonderfully good. Never in his life had he partaken of so rich and delicious a meal. He ate hastily, uneasily, his eyes following the girl as she moved with a quick gliding motion about him, taking away the empty bowls, supplying him with freshly filled ones, though where she got them he was at a loss to know.

At last when he had eaten his fill he arose and bowed again. "I am more than grateful to you for this meal, fair damsel," said he, "and now I must continue on my journey." For again there had fallen upon him a feeling of danger, a panic desire to get away.

"Not so fast! Not so fast, young woodcutter!" hissed the girl. "Neither now nor ever will you leave this hut alive. For long years I have waited for this moment. Now I shall have my revenge!"

Kil Tong leaped back with a cry of terror. The face and form of the creature before him changed in the twinkling of an eye. The body grew long and coiled itself up, the feet and arms vanished, the face shrank and flattened and became unmistakably the head of a snake with forked tongue flicking venomously.

"Yes-s," hissed the voice. "I am the ghost of the serpent you killed long ago. My time for vengeance has come at last. Prepare to die!" She drew back as if about to lunge at him.

Kil Tong fell on his knees in an agony of fright, praying for his life, and so effectual were his words that the creature hesitated. Then with a mocking laugh she bade him rise.

"One chance I will give you," said she, "yet it is scarcely a chance. Rather it will give me the joy of watching you suffer longer." She paused.

Kil Tong rose to his feet. He was trembling still but his panic fears seemed to have grown quieter. "If a man has a chance of saving his life," said he, "that at least is better than to die like a rat in a hole. Tell me, what way are you opening by which there is a possibility of escape?"

"Not exactly a possibility," said the snake with a cruel laugh. "Listen to what I say. Somewhere, lost in the woods behind this hut, is an ancient Buddhist temple wherein hangs a deep-toned bell. No one has rung that bell, no one has heard it ring, for more than a century. If you, by any impossible magic art, any means whatsoever, can cause that gong to sound its ancient note at the hour of midnight, then you shall go free."

"The night is still young!" cried Kil Tong hopefully. "Let me attempt this task." He would have rushed to the door of the hut but the snake-woman writhed in front of him, barring his way. She fixed her small unblinking eyes upon him, forcing him back to where he had been.

"The bell must ring while you stay here, unmoving." The voice was scarcely a whisper. "Bend your too confident knees! Sit down at once!"

Kil Tong sank upon the floor, all power of motion taken from him. He felt as if his muscles were made of cotton. His shoulders sagged, his head drooped.

Moments went by . . . then hours . . . time was not. The serpent stared unblinkingly into his eyes. He could not move, he could not think.

Suddenly, clear and strong on the night air, came the deep vibrant tones of a bell. Twelve times it struck. Before the last one sounded the snake-woman, with a piercing shriek, vanished and Kil Tong lay alone on the floor of a deserted hut.

The next morning the young woodcutter awoke refreshed

and rested and fully resolved to find the temple and the bell
which had saved his life by its timely ringing. He had not far
to search. In the depth of the woods behind the hut he came
upon a small ruined building half covered with vines and
the encroaching forest growths. The walls were broken and
fallen but the tower in which the great bell hung still stood
untouched by time or decay. Kil Tong climbed into it and
looked curiously about, wondering who or what could have
swung the heavy clapper against that great bronze bell.

A little sound, a flutter, a cry, he scarce knew what, drew
his attention, and in a corner of the open tower he saw two
huddled pheasants. He looked again at the bell and saw that
it was stained with blood. Then he understood.

Very tenderly Kil Tong leaned over the injured pheasants
whose breasts were bruised and torn by their impact upon the
bell. "Poor grateful ones!" he whispered. "It was you who
saved me from a frightful death and now are near dead your-
selves. Greatly have you overpaid your small debt to me for
my protection these many years past!"

With skillful fingers he bound up their wounds with cotton
cloth torn from his own clothing. Nor did he leave them until they were able to raise their heavy bodies on beating wings
and fly away.

In due time Kil Tong found his way out of the forest and
lived the rest of his life uneventfully. Only once in a while
when the mood was upon him would he tell to chosen friends
his strange adventure with a vengeful serpent-ghost and two
grateful pheasants.

7. THE MAN WHO FEARED NOTHING

HWANG was the strongest man in the village of Wang-
sim-ri albeit he was oldish, thirty-four or so. He lifted
with ease the heaviest weights, and the thrust of his muscular
arm might well make the bravest and sturdiest tremble. But

rarely did anyone have reason to be afraid in his presence, for Hwang was as good-natured as he was strong and much beloved by his fellow villagers. Moreover he did not know what fear was and laughed at dangers that made other men's limbs grow weak as water. Even ghosts held no terrors for him, though in truth he had never actually seen one.

It happened one summer day that the people of Wangsim-ri were gathered together, picking melons in a field nearby. A holiday spirit was upon them, they ate the good yellow fruit almost as fast as they picked it, and they laughed and joked among themselves, poking fun now and then at Hwang, who, though so mighty in body, was not very strong as to intelligence.

In the midst of the clear gay afternoon clouds began to gather; the face of the sun became hidden and thunder rumbled. Blacker and blacker grew the sky, forked lightning shot through the inky clouds toward the earth, followed almost on the instant by a ripping, tearing sound and then a roaring crash. It seemed as if the whole world were about to be torn apart. Rain fell in blinding sheets; wind rattled in the bamboo grove and lashed the tops of the trees, and now and again it seemed as if a ball of fire fell from the air and went rolling over the fields.

The villagers scattered, screaming, to whatever shelter they could find, drenched to the skin already. A number of them gathered in an old forsaken temple shrine whose overhanging roof, upturned at the corners, kept the downpour from falling directly on their unprotected heads.

"By the soul of my ancestor," said one, his teeth chattering in terror, "all the evil spirits in the world must have got loose with intent to destroy us!"

"Ghosts will walk," cried another. "Even the most secret and fortunate graves will break open as a result of all this violence."

"And goblins will have power and opportunity to do all manner of harm," said a third. "Truly it would be well if we stayed together for protection and kept within this shelter once sacred to an ancient god."

Hwang, alone of all the villagers, was neither terrified nor cautious. "Why should anyone fear?" said he boastfully. "What is a summer storm to me? Or ghosts or goblins or spirits of evil, for that matter? I am not afraid!" and he beat his brawny breast and strutted about with his head high.

At that moment a terrific flash of lightning and immediate roar of thunder broke over their heads. Everyone fell flat on his face and began to mumble charms and incantations. But not Hwang; he stood with folded arms, leaning against the broken wall of the shrine, and laughed as the rain, blowing in, ran off his chin and dripped onto his cotton coat.

When there was a momentary lull in the storm someone leered up at Hwang. "Since you are such a daredevil, friend Hwang, let us set you a task which will show up your folly and hollow boasting!" He consulted with some of the others who gathered around him, then made a proposition.

"Go now," said he, "while the storm rages. Pass into Seoul by the Water Gate, to the southwest, cross the city to the east entrance, and there climb to the upper story of the gate and hammer three large nails into the beam of its roof.

Thereby we shall know you have been to the place when we follow, anon, after the storm has abated."

The villagers all nodded approval and many of them smiled tauntingly. "That will prove whether you have courage or no," they said.

"Come now, will you accept the challenge?" said he who had proposed it.

Hwang gathered up some loose nails from the crumbling walls of the shrine, found a stone to use as a hammer and without a word stepped out into the rain. He turned to wave and grin at them good-naturedly enough. Then another blinding streak of lightning and uproar, followed by rain more violent than ever, seemed to envelop him, and the villagers could not see him any more. They sighed as they turned to one another again.

"He is a good sort," they said, "even if he is boastful and a little stupid. Perhaps we should not have sent him into such danger."

Meanwhile there was Hwang striding along toward the Water Gate, his straw sandles swishing, his sodden clothes clinging to his wet body and the rain running in rivers off his hat and chin. Thunder still roared and the lightning flashes in the black clouds were more constant than ever. Hwang did not care. He blinked the rain out of his eyes and shook it off his shoulders as he saw the tall gate looming in front of him.

The streets of Seoul were entirely deserted and there was nothing whatever to delay his quick passage to the East Gate. Once there he climbed quickly up the steps to the upper story.

He took his three nails and began to hammer them into a beam of the wall. In the midst of a stroke he paused and caught his breath. The interior of the tower was almost dark, but he had glimpsed something which made even his dauntless heart stand still. Hanging from a crossbeam high up above his head was a swaying white figure. It was slim and hung limp, and Hwang's first and very natural thought was that it was a ghost, abroad and visible in this frightful storm.

A gust of wind caught and shook the creature, and Hwang thought he heard a faint moan. With hands that trembled he finished hammering in the third nail and turned to hurry down the steps. Then he stopped.

"By the soul of my grandmother!" said he aloud. "What am I, the fearless Hwang, about that I should flee from a ghost in terror? I will go to the creature and address it."

He climbed up closer to the beam from which hung the shadowy white object and then gasped in astonishment, for it was neither ghost nor goblin but a young maid hanging by her hair!

Quickly Hwang worked his way out upon the beam, released the girl and got her down, where she lay as if lifeless. He gathered rain water in his great hands, dashed it in her face and at length revived her. She sat up, gazing at him in bewilderment.

Hwang bowed courteously. "Fair maid," said he, "how came you here in this sad state, and who are you? The daughter of some great scholar or magistrate, I am sure, for your silken clothes and delicate face betoken such to be the case."

"Strange Sir," she answered, "let me first thank you for

restoring me to life. I am, as you guess, the daughter of a high official here in Seoul. But how I came to be thus hanging by my hair from a beam in the East Gate, I cannot tell you."

"Doubtless some evil goblin played this trick upon you," Hwang suggested, his brows darkening with anger.

"Indeed that must have been the case. I was disporting myself in the garden of my home when the storm came. Then, as I was running to the house, rough hands caught me up and bore me through the air with such speed that I lost consciousness. When I came to for a moment I found myself in the position in which you discovered me, and then I suppose I fainted again."

"Would that I might meet that goblin!" declared Hwang, clenching his fists.

"Nay," said the girl, "waste no time or thought on revenge, but take me quickly to my father. I will show you the way, and he will reward you with a generous hand."

So, with great gentleness in spite of his powerful strength, Hwang assisted the girl down the steps of the gate and bore her swiftly through the pouring rain to her home.

On the way they became somewhat acquainted. Hwang learned that she was called Nim Tori-si and was the daughter of Nim Pansu. He told her his name and village and how he had chanced to be climbing to the upper story of the East Gate in the midst of a frightful storm.

They found the home of Nim Pansu in a state of great commotion because of the girl's disappearance. Hwang would have slipped away unnoticed in the clamor of rejoicing and thanksgiving if Nim Tori-si herself had not insisted on presenting him to her father. Both parents besought him to be their guest and treated him with the utmost consideration while he stayed with them.

The long and the short of it all was that the parents at length proposed a marriage between the two. It was quite unusual in that Hwang's station in life was far below that of the lady and he had no parents to make the proper arrangements. It was whispered that Nim Tori-si herself had prevailed upon her parents. As for Hwang, he was bewildered by the grandeur of the house and the high state of the family, and allowed himself to be led about without quite realizing what was going on.

"We shall make a scholar of our son-in-law," declared Nim Pansu, "and there is no better time to begin than now."

So Hwang was set in the midst of many volumes of the Chinese classics and bidden to read this and memorize that until he grew not only bewildered but well nigh frantic. His strength oozed out of him, his fearlessness deserted him, and he became a timid and haunted creature.

In the meantime the villagers of Wang-sim-ri waited in vain for the return of their strong one. Finally they set out for Seoul and found the three nails hammered into the beam of the East Gate but no sign of Hwang. They were unhappy about the matter for, though they teased him, they admired his strength, his fearlessness and his good nature.

And then they found him! A group of them were fishing in the river when they saw a small punt zigzagging back and forth in a crazy manner. When they drew closer they saw Hwang sitting alone with a pile of books before him and an empty clam bag on his head. He would scull vigorously for a few moments, then grasp a book and pore over it, muttering to himself, "Confucius says this; no, Confucius says that—but the Chinese sages—alas, I know not at all what any of them say!" Then tears would flow down his cheeks and he would shiver as if in a chill.

"Poor soul, he has gone quite mad!" said one of the villagers.

"You know the cure?" said another.

"Aye, but who would dare try such a cure on such a one as Hwang?"

They argued among themselves and at last a young man, strong and full of courage, agreed to see what he could do. He rowed himself close to the punt and jumped in. Seizing Hwang by the hair, he slapped him three times, stamped three times with his left foot and spat three times over the side of the boat. That, as everyone knew, was the way to drive the demons of madness out of a man. Then he got ready to jump into the river and swim, if Hwang proved violent.

But Hwang merely looked at him, a light dawning in his eyes as if he were just coming to himself after a period of unconsciousness. Then he uttered a shout of triumph, thumped on his big chest with his large fists and cried out, "Oh my friends! my fellow villagers! I have suffered many things but now I am going back with you to Wang-sim-ri and never leave it any more! Ha! I am already brave again! I am not afraid of anything! Anything at all!"

"Not even ghosts?" shouted one of the villagers to him.

"No, not even ghosts and goblins!" Hwang paused a moment and his face grew thoughtful. "There is one thing and one only that I do fear—that I shall always be afraid of."

"What is that?" cried the villagers.

"Learning!"

8. KEEL-WEE, A KOREAN RIP VAN WINKLE

LONG, long ago when King Wang was ruler of Korea there lived in a northern province a woodcutter, Keel-Wee by name, with his wife and family. They had a small grass-roofed house on the edge of the village, a little land and a large, strong, gentle bull. Keel-Wee loved the bull almost as much as he did his wife and children, perhaps more, for his wife was the daughter of Kim-Gee, a very important person, and she never let anyone forget that fact. She was a grumbling, scolding, discontented soul and made life at home rather miserable for Keel-Wee, always nagging him, calling him lazy and good-for-nothing, and blaming him because there was never quite enough to eat in the house. As for the children, he really knew very little about them for it is not always customary for a Korean father to become really intimate with his sons and daughters.

So Keel-Wee took great satisfaction in the company of Obong, his faithful, plodding bull. Never was there a gentler or friendlier beast. He would look at his master with large kindly eyes, nuzzle against him with his moist nose and breathe into his face, a breath that smelled of hay and meadow flowers. Then his master would gently scratch around the back of his ears. There was a white mark around the left one which made him handsome and distinguished-looking, Keel-Wee thought. The children loved him, too, rode on his back and pulled him around by his horns. He was used to children and let them do what they would with him as a rule, only walking away with a snort of reproof when they became too rough. That would put them in their place. But for Keel-Wee he had nothing but love, and wherever the man was, Obong was pretty sure to be following close at his heels.

Now it happened one morning that Keel-Wee's wife was particularly scolding and out of sorts and his children noisy and quarrelsome. He sighed with relief when he closed the door of his house behind him and went out in the yard to find his friendly beast. He fastened his woodcutting tools upon the broad and willing back and started off for the mountains to get a load of fuel. For long hours the two plodded along together at an easy gait. Every year the village woodcutters were obliged to go farther up into the hills because the forests nearby had been completely stripped of trees and no one took any pains to cut sparingly and leave enough young growth to reforest. Keel-Wee did not mind. The farther he got from home and the longer he could stay, the better pleased he would be, or so he thought at the moment.

They went on and up, deeper and deeper into the uncut wooded mountains. At long last they came to a slight clearing. Keel-Wee laid a restraining hand on the bull's flank and they both stopped and looked around them.

They had never been in that particular spot before. Through the thinning trees the man could see the peaks of mountains rising above him. At one side a view opened out over the green valley from which he had come, and, in among the low evergreens and hardy mountain oaks close around him, boulders jutted from the earth, giving the surface of the land a wild and rugged appearance. A keen air blew about him, lifting his somber mood and making him feel happy and excited.

After taking off his wide-brimmed horsehair hat and his cotton jacket, Keel-Wee seized his ax and was about to wield it with sure stroke against the tall straight tree standing near him when his eye was caught by a strange sight. A few paces away from him, half hidden by underbrush, two men were sitting on boulders, playing at changki (chess). It was odd, certainly, that anybody should be playing a game out here on the mountain and with so much absorption. But what struck Keel-Wee with particular amazement was the clothing of the two, which was very rich and beautiful and in the style worn by noblemen in the Chow dynasty some two thousand years before.

Keel-Wee approached the players quietly. He noticed that their skin was wax white, that their hands were long and thin, and, as the sunlight fell through a rift in the trees full upon them, he saw that they cast no shadow. Very evidently they were from the kingdom of spirits, the land of enchantment and wonder. He was about to draw back, seize the leading rope of Obong and flee down the mountainside, when he noticed one of the players making a move that was undoubtedly a poor one. He drew closer and, watching over the shoulder of the nearer of the ghostly players, he became absorbed in the game. Another foolish move was made. Keel-Wee cried out impulsively, "Don't move your man there! You'll lose him. Better to check that and that!"

The two strange creatures ceased playing for a moment and looked at Keel-Wee steadily and mysteriously. His breath stopped and he felt as if a powerful spell were working upon him so that he could no longer move. It soon passed, however, and he looked questioningly again at the two. Though they did not smile or say anything they seemed to convey the idea that they meant to be friendly. One of them drew a small brass box from the depths of his flowing sleeve, opened it and took out a seed, which he placed in Keel-Wee's hand, indicating that he should put it in his mouth. Keel-Wee did so and felt his jaws clamp shut so that he could no longer open them.

The two players resumed their game and the woodcutter went on watching. Once again he was so disturbed at a move that was made that he tried to speak out. Finding that he could not open his mouth, he reached forward and took the chessman in his hand. He promptly received a sharp rap on his knuckles, but still the ghostly creatures showed no signs of anger or unfriendliness. One of them almost smiled.

Keel-Wee stuck his ax handle upright in the ground, rested his chin on the head of it and watched and watched. Hours went by. He was not aware of time, and for the two from the spirit world time did not exist. Keel-Wee leaned more heavily on his ax and went on watching. . . .

Suddenly the wood of the ax handle gave way, dissolved into ashes. Keel-Wee lost his balance and fell sprawling forward. He knocked the game board and the chessmen onto the ground. When he rolled over and started to pick himself up, they had vanished completely. So had the strange shadowless players, and so had Keel-Wee's bull.

He found it absurdly hard to get on his feet again, for his joints were stiff and painful. His hand became tangled in a thin, straggly beard which had most certainly not been on his chin when he had left home that morning. And it was white! So was the long hair that had broken from his tightly bound top-knot and fallen down over his shoulders. His clothes were in such rags they barely covered him, and the shreds of the hat and coat he had discarded were half buried in dead leaves and underbrush.

Keel-Wee was thoroughly bewildered, and most of all by the fact that Obong had strayed away. Never before had the faithful beast deserted him. He looked about and then decided the creature must have wandered home, and he would do likewise.

The trees of the forest seemed strangely tall and the trail by which he had come up the mountain was overgrown and hard to follow. But at last he made his way down to the village and entered it through the age-old wall by the gate of the tall painted idol. *That* was not changed, nor were the contours of the hills around the valley, but all else looked as different to Keel-Wee as if he had dropped into a new world.

The streets seemed to him very foreign and strange and they were full of people who stared. Little boys laughed and threw stones at him, calling him "Old Mountain Daddy." There was not a familiar face to be seen anywhere.

At last, growing more and more bewildered and unhappy, he passed a gentle, friendly-looking person with a servant walking behind him with books. Evidently this man was a scholar. Keel-Wee bowed himself to the ground, and as he did so the seed fell out of his mouth.

"If you please, Honorable Stranger," said he, his own voice sounding unfamiliar in his ears and almost as if it had grown rusty, "will you tell me where the house and family of one Keel-Wee may be found and—and his wife who is the daughter of Kim-Gee?"

The man first looked puzzled, then a gleam of understanding appeared in his face. "Ah, ancient one," said he, "you must indeed have come from far to ask after people so long dead and in forgotten tombs. There was once a noted yang-ban—a nobleman—by the name of Kim-Gee who lived in this town. But that was a hundred years or more ago. It seems to me I remember an old story that a daughter of his married a woodcutter who strayed off into the mountains and was eaten by a tiger."

"I assure you, nothing could be further from the truth!" cried Keel-Wee indignantly. "I myself am that same son-in-law to Kim-Gee and am just returning after a day of wood-cutting in the mountains—or at least—" Remembering that he had not really cut any wood in all his long day of watching the ghosts at their game, he hesitated and became confused.

The man smiled, touched his forehead significantly and shook his head to the small crowd that had gathered around them. Keel-Wee said no more but moved on.

He spoke to others, seeking to find the location of his old home. At last he came upon it, or at least he thought it was the spot where his grass-roofed hut had once been. The look of the hills round about was familiar, and the turn of the road. No house stood there now, however, only an empty meadow. But, oh joy of joys! there, lazily chewing his cud, stood Obong—or if it was not Obong himself it was the exact and perfect duplicate of his beloved bull! Keel-Wee approached him in trembling eagerness. The animal turned large kindly eyes upon him and put a moist nose into his outstretched hand. It was! It *was* Obong, and as final proof there was a white mark around his left ear!

Keel-Wee embraced him joyfully. "Come," said he, "we have been too long in this world, you and I. Let us hurry away to the hills where the ghost men play their games and cast no shadows. Age has come upon us without our knowing it, but what does that matter? We are together again!"

Now whether this bull was indeed Obong or his great-great-many-times-great-grandson, no one knows, nor does it much matter. He moved with languid gait, easily and contentedly, beside Keel-Wee, out of the town grown so large and strange, up into the mountains that never change. And from that day to this no man has ever seen either of them!

9. THE MAGIC AMBER

THERE once was an old man named Ki-Tsze. He lived all alone in a small hut on the bank of the river Han, alone, that is, except for his dog Bo-dug and his cat Yawa. The three were great friends and understood one another, though what language they used has since been forgotten, for that was very many years ago. In those days cats and dogs were not enemies but friendly with each other, though Bo-dug, of course, felt that he was altogether superior to any cat, and no doubt Yawa had the same opinion regarding herself and any dog.

Ki-Tsze sold wine to the travelers who passed his door, and to the ferrymen who plied a boat across the river nearby, and to neighbors who came to him with their narrow-necked bottles. These he filled from his own jars, and people said that no one in the whole world sold sweeter wine or gave the buyer a fuller measure for his money. Everyone liked Ki-Tsze though it was not his habit to talk much. When he did he was soft-spoken and gentle in what he said.

Bo-dug and Yawa both loved him and were very careful of him, helping him find things when he misplaced them, which he often did, being very absent-minded. They saw to it that he fed himself and them regularly, and on cold evenings they kept him warm as he sat over his small fire box, the cat curled up on his shoulder, the dog lying close at his side.

All went well with the three of them until one autumn when a long drought destroyed the garden crops, dried up the neighboring rice paddies, and neither villager nor traveler had money with which to pay Ki-Tsze for his fine sweet wine.

He never refused anybody who came with an empty wine bottle, however, or hesitated a moment to give to a tired, discouraged-looking traveler the wine that he knew would refresh him.

" 'Tis good wine," he would say. "I made it myself. It is neither too strong nor too weak. It will lift the heart. As for the payment, you will give me the money when times are easy again and there is food a-plenty for all. Until then, no matter."

Bo-dug and Yawa did not approve of that way of doing business and they approved still less when the food their master gave them grew skimpier and skimpier. They talked the matter over together but there did not seem to be anything they could do about it. When they showed their disapproval to Ki-Tsze, he merely shrugged his shoulders.

"I shall be paid in time," he said. "So long as my wine is good and gives strength and well-being to those who drink it, we have nothing to worry about."

Finally there came a day when the last jar sounded hollow and almost empty and there was not a single string of coins left that would buy the material to make more wine, nor yet food for the three friends to live on, nor fuel for their fire box. Even Ki-Tsze was downhearted, though he said nothing about it.

That evening they sat huddled together on the floor, which was bitter cold, for, of course, there were no flues under the flagged stones to warm them, as in rich men's houses. The flatbottomed ferry boat had long been moored, neighbors had gone to bed and the desolate road in front of the hut would surely carry no travelers in the black of the cold, starless night. Ki-Tsze, Bo-dug and Yawa dozed and shivered.

Suddenly they were awakened by a knocking on their bamboo door. The man started, stretched, shook himself free of his animal friends and got stiffly and groaningly to his feet. When he opened the door a tall man bent his head to avoid the low lintel and stepped over the doorsill into the room. A great gust of wind blew in after him, which was strange, as Ki-Tsze had noticed how quiet the night was.

The stranger wore the usual wide-brimmed horsehair hat with the narrowing crown, tied down securely over his top-knot. He had on a heavily padded cloak, and his boots with the upturned toes were new and shiny. He is probably a yangban, thought Ki-Tsze. Surely he will have plenty of money to pay for my wine. He bowed deeply.

"Honorable Sir," said he, "you have doubtless come to this my miserable hut to taste of the wine I have made with my own poor unskillful hands." In spite of the humble way in which he spoke, which was the proper and mannerly way for any man to speak to his betters, there was a hint of satisfaction in the look of his eyes for he was justly proud of his wares.

"It is true," the stranger answered, "that I am desirous of sampling a jug of the wine for which you are famous, but you must understand that I have not so much as a penny wherewith to pay you. Out yonder on the dark road I was waylaid and robbed. I have barely escaped with my life. If you in kindness will refresh me with a cup of your life-giving brew, I will thank you for your charity but can give you no money in return."

Ki-Tsze smiled happily. There was nothing that pleased him more than praise for that which he made with such care. "Think not of payment at all," said he. "It is my privilege and great honor to serve you—" He stopped short, remembering with horror that he might not even have so much as one jugful of his precious wine left in the last jar.

Bo-dug growled resentfully and Yawa looked at the

stranger with disapproving green eyes. But neither of the men paid any attention to them.

Ki-Tsze set a bowl on a small lacquer table on the floor and the tall man knelt, then sat upon his heels before it. Holding his breath in his anxiety, the wine merchant poured from his last jar, tipping it up and up until not a single drop more would run out. The stranger's bowl was but half full.

"Fetch another jar," said the man somewhat impatiently.

"Ai-goo!" murmured Ki-Tsze, blushing with shame. "Alas, this is all I have! There is no more wine, no, not one drop more, in my house, and nothing wherewith to make a fresh supply. Truly, I am sorry beyond measure not to be able to give you more."

The man laughed harshly. " 'Tis evident you meant not the charitable words you spoke and intend to keep your wine for those who can pay for it!" He leaped to his feet and started indignantly toward the door.

"Oh no, *no,* good Sir," cried Ki-Tsze, stepping in front of him. "You mistake me utterly. You are my guest—I rejoice to give you all that I have—but—but—" He covered his face with his hands. "In shame I say it—I have no more."

There was a long moment of silence, and when Ki-Tsze dropped his hands and looked into the stranger's face he was astonished. It bore a friendly, understanding look and there was something shining and not-of-this-world about it.

"Give me your wine jar," the man said in a gentle tone. "Look you!" He spread out one hand, and Ki-Tsze saw in it a round piece of yellow amber. This the man slipped into the mouth of the wine jar.

"Now," said he, "pour. There will be plenty." And when Ki-Tsze looked into the jar it was full to the brim!

After that things went well for the three. The wine merchant's jar never became empty no matter how much he poured out of it. He never replenished it, yet there it was, always a whole full jar of gleaming sparkling wine, and better than the best that he had ever made.

Neighbors, travelers, and ferrymen flocked to his door and, in a very short time, people were able to pay again. Strings of cash were laid by in a chest and Bo-dug and Yawa as well as Ki-Tsze grew fat and prosperous. Winter and summer went by.

Then trouble came knocking at their door again. The old wine merchant had had a rush of business. Over and over he had filled the narrow-necked bottles of his customers from his ever-full jar containing the magic amber, and always his jar had refilled itself. Then suddenly, to his utter astonishment, he found it completely empty. Not a single drop remained, and when he shook it there was no rattling of the amber against its earthenware sides.

What had happened was plain enough. Ki-Tsze realized at once that in filling one of the wine bottles he must have poured out the talisman with the wine and some one of his customers had unwittingly gone off with it. But which one? He tried to remember the names of those he had served in the last day or two. Most of them had been neighbors. It should not be very difficult to find the man who had a bottle that never had to be refilled, and reclaim his treasure.

But that was more easily thought of than carried

out. Ki-Tsze made the rounds of the village and country-side, telling of his loss. He asked the ferrymen and bade them inquire among their passengers, for many of them crossed the river every day. It was no use. Either the magic amber had fallen into the bottle of a traveler who had not returned, or else whoever had found it was saying nothing about it and intended to keep it for himself.

After a while hard times fell once more upon the three friends. The strings of money were all gone, food became scarce and there was nothing with which to buy more. Bo-dug and Yawa decided it was time they took matters into their own hands. They talked the matter over.

"That piece of yellow amber had a certain smell to it," declared Bo-dug, wrinkling his nose as if he had already caught the scent of it.

"Yes," agreed Yawa, "and there was a shininess about it. I put my eye to the wine jar once and saw it gleaming at the bottom of the liquid."

"We ought to be able to find it. Our poor old master is likely to starve if we don't help him. We must never fail him." The dog shook his shaggy head.

"And *we* shall starve too," added the cat mournfully.

After much discussion the two decided on a plan. They would search carefully through all the huts and plots of ground belonging to the neighbors and villagers. No one would be suspicious of a cat and a dog snooping around the premises. Bo-dug would attend to the out of doors. It might well be that the talisman had been dropped and lost. Yawa would take care of the houses, climbing onto the rafters and poking into the thatched grass roofs where someone might have hidden it, and peering into all chests and bottles that might contain it. They would know by the smell and by the faint shining when they had come anywhere near it.

They began their search at once and were very thorough about it. After a few weeks there was not a nook or cranny in anybody's house round about that had not received a visit from Bo-dug and Yawa with their keen nostrils and observant eyes. It was all of no use. Not a sight nor a smell of the missing amber did the two friends find.

Then they went further afield and finally crossed the Han river on the thickening ice that had already formed on the water. There they continued their search up and down the river bank. But still they were unsuccessful.

At long last Yawa, climbing noiselessly about in a grass-roofed hut beside the Han, saw a faint dim light coming, apparently, from the top of a tall chest. She sprang up and there discovered an old soapstone box from a crack in which issued a small thin line of brightness. She got the scent of it, too, the odd, unmistakable smell of the magic amber. Quivering with excitement, she tried to pry open the lid with her sharp teeth but it was tightly fastened down. Then she shoved the box with her paws so that it would fall off the chest and Bo-dug might be able to carry it off in his big mouth. But it was too heavy for her to move. Yawa jumped down and ran out to consult with Bo-dug. Fortunately the owner of the house was away so they had time to discuss the matter fully.

"There are rats in the thatch of the roof," said the cat.

"Perhaps a rat could gnaw a hole in the box and get the amber out."

"But would any rat do a favor for us who are the natural enemies of all their kind?" objected the dog.

"We might call for a meeting of the rats and mice and promise them we would not attack them—"

"For ten whole years!" finished Bo-dug as Yawa hesitated. "Excellent, my friend! You have a keen mind even if you are only a cat!"

Yawa gave him a disdainful look out of her round green eyes but she only said, "Go, summon the king of the rats if you know where to find him!"

Now the long and the short of the matter was that the king was found, the meeting called and the agreement quickly made. A committee of rats was appointed to gnaw a hole in the soapstone box, which was a hard task and took time, especially as it had to be done at night or when the owner of the house was safely out of the way. When at last there was a small opening the tiniest mouse in the community was chosen to crawl in and fetch the precious amber out. The little creature, once in the box, could not move the talisman and had to call for help. Mice came scampering from all over the grass roof, and finally after much shoving, hauling, squeaking and chattering the amber was gotten out, rolled to the edge of the chest and dropped onto the floor. Yawa seized it in her mouth and ran out. Bo-dug gave her an approving look and they both hurried silently and quickly to the river.

There they were met by a fresh difficulty, one that looked

impossible to overcome. When they had crossed the Han it had been winter and the water frozen so that they had been able to run across on the ice with no trouble at all. Now it was late spring, so long had they been busy trying to recover their master's treasure. The ice had melted and the lazily flowing river lay wide and deep between them and their home.

"Ai-goo!" exclaimed Yawa, spitting the amber out of her mouth. "By the soul of my grandmother, this is the end! We can in no wise cross the river, and I, for one, am weary of this task. No doubt our old master is dead of starvation by this time, anyway."

"For shame to think such a thing!" cried Bo-dug indignantly. "He is wiser than we and has no doubt picked up some kind of a living—even as we have. But he is old and very poor and we have found the treasure that will make him rich again. Do you suppose for a moment that I am going to fail him just because a river stands in my way?"

"Well, what do you propose doing?" the cat asked grumpily. "I can't swim. What is more, I don't like to get my feet wet."

"Do as I tell you," commanded Bo-dug, "and all will yet be well. Take the amber in your mouth again, climb on my back and fasten your claws in the thick ruff of fur around my neck—but don't scratch my face!"

Yawa did as she was bidden but with rather an ill grace. Then Bo-dug stepped into the river and began to swim. It was difficult going against the current and with the heavy cat on his back weighing him down, but he struggled on, breathing hard, swimming strongly. They had almost reached the opposite shore when a shout startled them. A boy running along the bank had caught sight of them and was pointing and screaming to his playmates to come and see the strange spectacle of a dog swimming across the river with a cat on his back.

Other children appeared. One of them began to laugh and then the others chuckled and laughed at the funny sight, some of them rolling on the ground with amusement.

Now laughter is more catching than the measles, and when Yawa saw and heard all that merriment going on, her sides began to shake, and she gurgled and choked with laughter herself. Finally, unable to keep her mouth shut another minute, she opened it with a burst of laughter and dropped the precious talisman into the stream.

Bo-dug saw it go and dove after it, plunging the cat under water with him. There was a short struggle, a churning up of river and mud, then he came to the surface again and made for the shore with Yawa's claws digging into his neck and Yawa herself sputtering and coughing, the most indignant cat in the whole of Korea!

Once on shore she continued to spit and sneeze. She fluffed out her bedraggled fur, and when she had got the water out of her lungs and mouth she flew at Bo-dug with her claws out and fury in her eyes.

"Idiot!" she cried. "Clumsy, good-for-nothing fellow! What do you mean by getting me wet with that horrid river water? Me, with my sleek coat and my daintiness! Don't you *know* I can't abide even the rain?" She spat and growled, more angry than ever, and her tail swelled to twice its natural size.

Bo-dug growled back. "What is a little wetting when you were fool enough to let our master's magic amber drop out of your mouth—and just because some silly children laughed? *Now* what are we going to do?"

"I know just what *I* am going to do," declared Yawa. "I am going off by myself and will take care of myself! And from now on, forever, when my kind sees any of your kind they will spit and growl and glare and their fur will stand up and their tails grow large and their claws will be out—as mine are now!"

And so it has been from that day to this and doubtless will always be, between cats and dogs—except when they have learned to know each other personally.

As for Bo-dug, he watched his friend walk haughtily away, her tail, still overlarge, held stiffly in the air. Then he settled himself on the bank of the river near where the amber had been lost. Day after day he stayed there, leaving the spot only long enough to hunt for a few scarce scraps to eat. All through the days and all through the nights he kept a faithful watch.

Finally there came a fisherman along the river bank. Bo-dug kept a careful eye on him as he fished. When he landed a large catch and hauled it flopping and struggling to the shore, the dog rushed over and seized the biggest fish in his mouth before the man could rescue it. Off he ran, with the fisherman shouting and storming behind him. Others followed in the chase, but Bo-dug stretched out his four legs and fairly flew over the ground. His mouth dripped saliva for the hunger that was in him, but he would not have eaten that fish if his life had depended on it. His nostrils quivered with the scent of the magic amber.

At last the men chasing him fell off, one by one, and Bo-dug left them all far behind. He slackened his speed and made his way by little lanes and back alleys, where he hoped no one would notice him, to the hut where his master lived.

Ki-Tsze was sitting in the doorway. He was thinner, older, more bowed and worn, but there was the same gentle look in his face. Bo-dug laid the fish at his feet and then wagged his tail almost off and uttered his joy and affection in every way that a dog can. The wine merchant took him in his arms, patted and praised him.

"So you have come back to your old friend," said he, "and brought me a fine big fish for my dinner! Come, I will clean it and cook it and we two will eat it, share and share alike. From the look of your lean sides I am sure you have had as little to fill your stomach these hard days as I have."

Anyone could guess the rest of the story; how the magic amber dropped out of the fish when the old wine merchant cut it open; how he ran to his empty wine jar, put the talisman in it with fingers that trembled; how the sparkling wine at once bubbled to the top of the jar! After that Ki-Tsze's fortune was made, and he took good care not to let his treasure slip away from him again. He and Bo-dug lived happily and comfortably to a ripe old age. As for Yawa, she foraged for herself and was never seen by the two friends again. Wild she became, and wild were her children and her children's children, and so are all her descendants in Korea even to this very day.

10. FATE AND THE FAGGOT GATHERER

KIM-KHODOURY was a poor man who earned a scanty living for himself and his wife by selling bundles of wood. Every other day he went into a nearby ancient forest, cut and gathered the dry, dead wood and carried it home on his back in a frame built for the purpose and called a jiggy. There he would bind it into bundles, one to be kept against the coming winter cold and two to be sold the next morning. The jiggy held just enough faggots for three good-sized bundles. Always Kim-Khodoury had two to sell and one to keep.

One morning, however, he found to his surprise only two

bundles where he had left three. Some thief must have made off with one, but it was strange that, having dared to steal one, he had not taken all. Kim-Khodoury sold the other two and the next day came back from the forest with faggots enough to bind into three, as usual. Again in the morning one had disappeared and two were left.

He made up his mind he would find out who the thief was by catching him in the act. So the next evening he left three fresh bundles in their accustomed place and hid in a dark corner of his kitchen to watch. The moon was full and shed a clear light over his yard, his small garden and the three bundles of faggots. No one could approach them without being seen.

The night wore on, and Kim-Khodoury began to be very sleepy, but he forced himself to stay awake, crouched uncomfortably though he was on the earthen floor in a corner of the kitchen court. At about midnight his eyelids drooped shut, but only for a moment. He pulled them open and stared at the faggots. One bundle had disappeared. There was not a sight or a sound of any living creature and the man was astonished beyond measure. He ran out and touched the two bundles as if he could not trust his own eyes. There were in very truth only two, and, in the bright moonlight, the land around him and the narrow road in front of his hut were completely bare and empty. It could not be—and yet it was. No one could possibly have got there and away again, and yet someone had.

The next time he left the faggots the same thing happened,

and the next. "It must be," muttered Kim-Khodoury, "that I close my eyes for longer than I think, and in that small moment some quick-footed, silent thief makes away with my wood." But he could scarce believe it possible.

Try as he would, however, he could not keep his eyes open all the time, especially at midnight, so he resolved to try a new plan. That evening he left only one bundle of faggots out beyond the cooking floor, and in the middle of that bundle he bound up himself. He was very uncomfortable but he had made up his mind that if his wood was taken this time he would go along with it.

In the dead of the night, without sound or any stirring about, the bundle of faggots, with Kim-Khodoury inside, rose straight up into the air. The astonished man, peeking through small open spaces between the pieces of wood, could see no form of anyone. It must be an evil spirit, he thought, bent on carrying him off to destruction, and he was terrified. The bundle, rocking slightly, passed through clouds; the stars burned large and bright and close to him, and he felt sure that his last moments of life had come.

Then the motion of the bundle grew slower, it bumped gently against something and came to rest. The man prisoned inside it trembled and waited. He heard voices, then hands fumbled with the cords binding the bundle, cut them, and the faggots fell apart.

Kim-Khodoury got shakily to his feet. He found himself standing on a cloud-washed shore. Dawn was breaking far below him and beside him stood several tall men dressed as

befitted servants of a wealthy prince. They were just as astonished to see him as he was to see them. Without a word of
explanation they seized him and hurried him off.

Before long they arrived at a gorgeous palace the walls of
which were of jade and crystal, the floors of marble and the
bamboo doors and window frames set about with precious
stones. Kim-Khodoury was taken into a throne room filled
with the perfume of flowering lotus and set down before a
kingly person in robes stiff with gold, on whose head rested a
crown glittering with diamonds.

He knelt and touched his forehead to the floor nine times,
as was fitting, then rose up but said nothing. What could he
say? Courtiers and servants, magistrates and politicians (no
doubt) milled around. They were dressed in green or sky
blue, not the usual white of a Korean, and they seemed taller
than mortal men. At last the king gave his attention to Kim-
Khodoury, asking who he was and why he was there. His explanation seemed to amuse his Supreme Highness.

"So you do not know that you now stand in the presence of
Okonchanté, high lord of the sky and ruler of men's desti-
nies?" said he, pleasantly enough. "Well, well, strange things
happen! The palace kitchens must have been short of wood.
I will pay you, Kim-Khodoury, for the faggots my servants
drew up from your yard, but the payment cannot be in strings
of cash—in mortal money. We have no use for such." He
dusted his hands together as if the mere thought of ordinary
coins was somewhat soiling to the touch.

Kim-Khodoury bowed again but could not find anything
to say.

"Let us see," King Okonchanté continued, "what fate has in store for you. Perhaps we can mend it a little." He snapped his fingers and a servant appeared immediately with a huge book in his hands.

The king riffled the pages, then opened to a certain one and read it. Kim-Khodoury watched breathlessly and finally, unable to bear the silence any longer, asked, "Your high and noble Majesty, Lord of the Sky, may it please you to let me know what you find about me in the Book of Destiny?"

"No vermicelli or rich rice—only watered soup," said the king, snapping the book closed. "I suppose you would like to change that."

Kim-Khodoury nodded his head vigorously.

"Then I shall have to borrow somebody else's fate and lend it to you. It won't be *your* destiny, remember, just loaned you until the owner comes to claim it."

"I scarcely understand your meaning, Honorable Sir." The poor man was more bewildered than ever.

King Okonchanté opened the Book of Destiny again, turned several pages, then smiled approvingly. "Ah, I have it. You, Kim-Khodoury, are to take upon you the fate of one Tchapogui until he asks for it. A good fate it is, rich, prosperous and altogether satisfying."

"But," interrupted Kim-Khodoury, "this man whose good destiny you are lending me—won't he be—ah—rather put out at my using it? What will he do without it and what shall I do when he takes it away from me?"

A titter of laughter ran through the throne room, greatly embarrassing the puzzled man. He noticed that many tall beautifully dressed courtiers had gathered in a semicircle around him. Their faces were kindly but they seemed to consider the proposed arrangement something of a joke. Kim-Khodoury wondered if the king was playing a trick on him for he, too, was laughing.

"Tchapogui may be a very fierce fellow," said the king. "I can scarcely tell yet. And he will certainly make great demands upon you, which you will have to meet."

Then, with the gentle laughter of King Okonchanté and his courtiers still in his ears, Kim-Khodoury felt himself lifted up off the marble floor, borne swiftly by unseen hands out of the beautiful jewel-bright palace and down through the air to the plot of ground where he was accustomed to lay his bundles of faggots.

His good fortune began at once and in a very natural way. The man to whom he sold his next two piles of wood gave him in return a larger bag of rice than he had expected. He sold half of it to a neighbor and with the price bought himself a little merchandise, which he again sold at a profit. Business grew fast and before long he and his wife were prosperous. They lived in a good house with a tiled roof and ample flues to carry heat from the outdoor kitchen under the flagstone floors, to keep them warm in winter.

Soon they had all they wanted that money could buy. They were healthy and still young, and yet they were not happy. Kim-Khodoury was haunted by fears. He could scarcely sleep at night and the good food his wife set before him was, oftener than not, taken away from him untouched. Always he carried in his mind the name Tchapogui, and he pictured

him as a strong and terrible man outraged that his good
destiny had been taken from him and determined to destroy
him, Kim-Khodoury, life and limb. It was a dreadful shadow
for a man to be living under. He was afraid to leave his house
lest he meet Tchapogui in the street, he denied himself food
for fear it had in some secret manner been poisoned by his
enemy (as he thought of him). He trembled at sight of a
stranger coming down the road and cried out in dismay if any
step crossed his veranda or any hand knocked at his door.

Now Kim-Khodoury's wife did the best she could to quiet
her husband's nerves, tried to cheer him up and change his
thoughts. But she had a sorrow of her own which she knew
was his sorrow also—or would have been if he were not
so completely taken up with his fear of Tchapogui. They
had no child and, as the years rolled on, they knew that no
son of theirs would ever come to fill their hearts with joy while
they lived and give respect and honor to their spirits after
they had gone to rest in their carefully selected tomb. So the
two sighed often and sometimes thought back with regret to
the days when they were poor and hungry but had no haunt-
ing fears and could still hope for a child to be born to them.

They were good to beggars, the two of them, and never
turned any who needed food or shelter from their door. One
day a strange-looking man and his wife came begging. They
were poorly clad and their faces were thin and worn, but Kim-
Khodoury, who happened to see them himself, decided they
looked different from the usual slovenly, ill-kempt crowd.
The woman kept well in the background and carried a bundle of something in her arms. Khodoury sent servants to give

them rice and kimchee, as much as they wanted, and to tell them to sleep the night in one of the out-buildings surrounding the courtyard. Then he forgot about them.

The next morning he woke early from a troubled sleep and went out on his veranda. He was startled to hear a wailing cry and, following the sound of it, he found a basket under an old broken down ox cart in his yard. Inside the basket, wrapped in clean padded cotton garments, lay a tiny child, a boy baby.

Kim-Khodoury lifted the small thing gently in his arms. The baby stopped crying and beat upon his chest with tiny fists and kicked strongly with his round little legs.

"Wife, wife!" cried Kim-Khodoury, running into the house. "See what those beggars have left us! A child! A boy as beautiful as the day!"

Anyone could guess what happened next in the story. Kim-Khodoury and his wife loved the little stranger from the moment they laid eyes on him. There was nothing to suggest whose the child was except perhaps for a single word scrawled on a thin piece of bamboo and wrapped in the coverings in which they found him. Kim-Khodoury could not read so he took it with him when he went before a magistrate to arrange for legally adopting him.

"What does it say?" he asked curiously.

" 'Tchapogui,' " replied the magistrate, looking at the fine brush-written characters. "That means 'left under a cart.' There is no doubt about the child's being in need of adoption."

But Kim-Khodoury was not listening to the last of the

magistrate's sentence. He had only heard the one word—Tchapogui. Suddenly he shouted with joy!

"Tchapogui!" he cried. "O wise, kind King Okonchanté! Most willingly I give back my happy destiny to my son! Home and two hearts have long been wanting him, preparing for him. Now he has come, and we are glad, glad!"

The adoption was soon completed and Kim-Khodoury hurried back to his wife. He held the child carefully, tenderly in his arms. "His name," said he to his wife, "is Tchapogui, a happy name, for now we shall live in great content, we three. We have our heart's desire and I have done with fear forever, for my destiny is one with the fate and good fortune of our son!"

11. THE THREE WISHES

KEN-TCHI and his wife once lived long ago in Korea. They were elderly, very poor, none too well and, to their great grief, childless. But they were good souls, kindly, humble, not given to grumbling. They made the best of what they had and did without cheerfully.

It happened one chilly autumn evening that they sat before their fire box dreaming of many things and saying little. At last Ken-Tchi took his yard-long pipe out of his mouth and sighed deeply.

"Wife," said he, "we are growing old and have no child to care for us in our age or to tend our burial place when we are gone. If we only had a son all my desires would be satisfied."

"Mine also," said the woman, whose name was Ok-San. "My heart is sick with longing for the feel of a small head against my breast. Life has deprived us of many things but if only—"

At that moment a white mist blew into the room, took form, and in a flash of light they saw standing before them a dazzling creature whom they realized at once was a damsel from the Heavenly Isles. They drew back in amazement, too startled to say a word.

"Have no fear, my good people," said the heavenly maid. "You have lived humbly and uncomplainingly until now, and although the seeds of discontentment have sown themselves in your minds this night, my mistress the Queen is minded to do you a great favor."

Ken-Tchi and his wife were still full of wonder, their mouths hanging open. The damsel continued, "Her Majesty has commanded me to grant you three wishes, anything your hearts may desire here or in that Other World of enchantment where she rules supreme. Guard your tongues, think carefully and, on the morrow at this time, I will come again and receive the answer from your own lips."

With that the white mist again surrounded her and she vanished, leaving only a sweet scent as of incense behind her.

"Well!" exclaimed Ken-Tchi at length. "Whoever heard of such a thing! Wife, we are made! There is nothing too great, too glorious or too precious for us to wish for!"

"Indeed yes!" agreed Ok-San. "And for that reason we must choose well and carefully."

Ken-Tchi put his chin in his hands and frowned thoughtfully. "Wealth," he suggested at length. "We have never had enough of anything."

"But what good will ropes of money be to us unless we have health and long life in which to enjoy it?" objected Ok-San.

"That would use up all three wishes, wealth, health and long life." Ken-Tchi counted them on his fingers. "Besides, what happiness can we find even in those if we have no child to share with us and inherit after we are gone?"

"If only we could have *four* wishes!" said Ok-San with a deep sigh. "Then we would have all that heart could desire!" She poked at the wood in the fire box discontentedly. "I'm hungry!" she grumbled. "I wish I had a juicy string of sausages, three feet long, to cook—"

Before she had finished her sentence a fat and handsome string of sausages fell out of the air at her feet—and there was the first wish already gone.

Ken-Tchi leaped up in fury. "Senseless one!" he cried. "By the soul of my maternal ancestor, you are more stupid than a pig! I wish that those miserable sausages were fastened to your nose!"

And immediately the greasy meat gathered itself together and flew to Ok-San's nose. No amount of pulling or tugging would get it off. Ok-San screamed and wept and jumped about in an agony of discomfort and fear. Ken-Tchi watched her angrily for a few moments, then his eyes softened.

"We have only one wish left," he mourned.

"But what happiness can I find in anything," moaned his wife, "if these dreadful sausages won't come off my nose?"

With that they both tried again to pull them off, then to cut them off, all to no avail. The horrid things could not be removed unless the nose was taken off with them.

"Very well," said Ken-Tchi bitterly, "here goes our chance for health, wealth and long life."

"Or a child," said Ok-San, weeping afresh. "I would rather have the child than all else."

Ken-Tchi merely grunted, then said in a loud tone, "I wish that these sausages would take themselves from the nose of my wife and vanish completely."

They were gone in the twinkling of an eye. Ok-San felt her nose carefully. It was as straight and smooth and clean as ever. (And it was a good-looking little nose; she had always been quite proud of it.) Then she dried her tears. "You might have left off that vanishing part of the wish," she said dolefully. "Then we would at least have had something to eat!"

They looked at each other in anger and then suddenly Ken-Tchi began to laugh. "So *stupid!*" he cried. "Both of us!"

"Ridiculous!" Ok-San was laughing too.

The more they looked at each other and thought of the whole absurd affair, the more they laughed. Tears came into their eyes, they held their sides and roared with laughter. They laughed so hard that the neighbors came in to see what it was all about. Then the neighbors laughed too, and slapped them on the back and thought they were a good sort when all was said and done, to be able to laugh at themselves.

At last everyone went home and Ken-Tchi and Ok-San lay down on their mats on the floor to go to sleep.

The next morning they were awakened early by a small wailing cry. Ok-San hurried to the door, and there on the clay porch she found a basket. Something alive and stirring was in it. A small fist waved in the air. Ok-San fell upon it with a cry of longing and delight.

And that is how Ken-wung-li came into the family of Ken-Tchi. Never was child so loved or so carefully reared, and never were there three souls so happy in each other's company. Perhaps Ken-wung-li was a motherless baby from another village. Ok-San didn't care where he had come from; he was *hers,* a gift from the Heavenly Isles, though she declared with humility that she didn't in the least deserve such good fortune. What was more, the other three gifts that Ken-Tchi and his wife had lost through their foolish thoughtlessness came modestly true. As time went on they had enough and to spare of the world's goods, good health to enjoy them and long, contented lives.

It may be that the Queen of the Isles of Enchantment was pleased that they could laugh at themselves and take life as they found it without discontent. Ken-Tchi sometimes wondered.

12. THE WIFE FROM ANOTHER WORLD

CHANG PY-ONG was a handsome youth who lived in a valley near the foot of a mountain. So high and steep and rugged was this mountain that no man had ever been known to climb it or even to cross the thick forests that surrounded it. Spirits, both good and bad, ghosts, genii and magic creatures were said to dwell in its clefts and wooded fastnesses. Great storms came thundering and rolling down from its snow-white peaks so often hidden in clouds, and the people of the straggling village at its foot looked at it fearfully with awe and wonder. But Chang Py-ong loved it. He liked to watch the cloud shadows racing across it on a windy day and, when the air was frosty clear in winter, he would gaze up at its glistening, faraway summit and smile and nod to it as to a friend.

Although he lived by himself except for one servant, and few ever sought him out in his lonely dwelling, he was a friendly person, kind, gentle, loving. It was a pity he had neither wife nor family.

Now it happened one day that a frightened stag came leaping across a clearing where he was engaged in raking up the early autumn leaves. The poor creature was breathing heavily, its eyes clouded with fatigue, and as it paused for a moment, the lad saw that its legs were trembling. He understood the situation at once; hunters were after the stag and it had almost reached the end of its strength.

"Poor thing!" cried Py-ong, and then as if it were human and could understand his words, he continued, "Come quickly and let me bury you in this pile of leaves till the hunters have ridden by."

While he spoke he made a hole in the great mound of leaves. The stag, seeming to grasp his thought at once, stepped into it and lay still. Chang Py-ong covered him up and then went on raking at a little distance.

Soon, with a clatter and commotion, three hunters burst into the clearing.

"Have you seen a stag running past this way?" cried one of them. "He must have been nearly done for. Did you catch sight of him?"

Py-ong leaned on his rake, regarding them slowly and

stupidly. Then he turned and pointed up the mountain side. "That is where the stags roam," said he, "but I would scarcely advise you to follow too far—"

"Indeed not!" agreed the hunter.

Another shrugged his shoulders. "If the stag has got as far as yonder mountain we had best give up and turn back. We have already come farther than is safe in this direction."

"No beast is worth an adventure with spirits," said the first, turning his horse about. "I wonder that *you* go on living so near that perilous mountain."

Chang Py-ong returned to his raking. "It is not so bad," said he, "so long as one stays here and minds one's own business."

After the hunters had gone the stag shook himself out of the pile of leaves and stood regarding the young man with soft, grateful eyes. Then amazingly the creature began to speak.

"Young Sir," he said, "you have saved my life and for that I am very thankful. Now I should like to do something for you in return."

Py-ong was still too much surprised to say anything and could only stare in silence.

The stag continued. "It is lonely for you here so near our haunted mountain, and high time for you to find yourself a wife and bind up your hair in token of the married state. Now if you will follow my directions exactly, you will win for yourself a lady who is not only beautiful but wise and tender beyond all earthly women. Shall I speak further of the matter?"

Chang Py-ong found his tongue at last. "By all means, strange creature, whatever you are. A man would certainly wish to win for himself so wonderful a wife."

The stag spoke again, his voice so clear and limpid that it seemed like the soft running of a brook over pebbles. "Beyond the thick forest that surrounds this mountain, up over a high ridge, lies a beautiful valley where there are eight spring-fed pools. Wide and deep and clear they are, and the lords of the mountain and skies draw water from seven of them. The eighth, the farthest away, is used by damsels of the spirit world to bathe and play in when the sun is warm. See then that you find these pools tomorrow. Wait not until the autumn chill deepens into frost. Go early and keep watch, hidden in the bushes that surround the eighth pool."

"But surely," interrupted Chang Py-ong, "it would not be seemly so to spy upon maidens from the Other World! Besides, the haunted mountain—"

The stag pawed the ground with a gesture of impatience. "Perhaps you are afraid," said he. "There *is* danger for any man who wanders and pries over yonder, without permission, but for one who is sent, as I am sending you— Besides, is it not worth taking a risk to win a beautiful and loving wife?"

Chang Py-ong nodded his head vigorously. "Yes—worth great risk. I pray you, forgive my interruption and go on with your instructions."

"The damsels will appear suddenly beside the pool. They will take off their white shining wings and place them carefully on the low branches of nearby trees. Then they will run into the pool and laugh and play together, shaking the water from their long black hair and from their silken garments. Note well the maid who pleases you most, then take her wings, fold them and hide them under your coat. When they have finished with their play they will put their wings upon their shoulders again and fly back to the spirit world whence they came."

"But—but"—again Chang Py-ong interrupted,—"do you suggest that by keeping her wings from her, I am to force this damsel to remain on earth and become my wife?"

The stag flicked his tail and stamped in evident annoyance. "And why not? Surely you are a slow and stupid mortal not to reach out eagerly and grasp this offer I am making you!"

"She—she—might not like such an arrangement."

"And since when has it been customary in Korea for a girl to be consulted about her marriage or even to see her husband before the wedding?"

The quiet, rippling tone of the stag's voice had taken on a harsher note. His proud antlered head was lifted high and his brown eyes had a fiery glint. Then suddenly he softened. "I am forgetting that I owe you my life," he said. "Put all your silly scruples aside and accept this gift that I am offering you without further question."

Chang Py-ong bowed his head meekly and the stag went on. "Without her wings the girl will not be able to fly back to her spirit home. She will follow you, and gladly, no doubt; you are very handsome—for a human. You will find in her, as I have said, a charming and affectionate wife. She will also be a careful housekeeper and a devoted mother to your children."

"And happy?" Chang could not help the whispered question.

"Usually happy, but not always," admitted the stag. "She will have times of homesickness when she will beg you, with sorrowful eyes, to let her see her white shining wings again, let her feel their softness on her shoulders if only for a moment. *Heed well my warning!* Do not let her once put on those wings of hers until after she has born you four children."

"You think by that time she will have forgotten her far-away home and be contented to stay with me?"

"No such thing!" snorted the stag. "No spirit being will ever be content to dwell on earth for long. But mothers are alike all the universe over. She would never leave a child behind her no matter how keen her desire to fly away. And even your slow human wits should tell you that though she could carry one child under each arm she could not carry three, much less four."

The stag turned and moved away in the direction of the mountain. Chang Py-ong ran after him. "You have not told me where to find these eight pools," said he, "except that they lie in a pocket of the hills over yonder."

"North, straight; over a ridge running parallel with the horizon; up and up and up, and then down into the valley." With that the stag broke into a long loping run and disappeared.

The next morning Chang Py-ong was up at dawn, ready to seek the adventure the stag had suggested to him. He walked north and soon came to the thickly forested foothills that lay between him and the haunted mountain. The long ridge stretching parallel with the horizon was easily found and crossed, but then his difficulties began. Sheer rock extended above him, up and up, with only an occasional jagged crack for a foothold and nothing whatever to cling to. However, Py-ong had the strength and determination of youth and was not unskilled in mountain climbing. After a long hard scramble he mounted the top of the cliff and looked out into a gorge, a deep pocket in the magic mountain. It was of surpassing loveliness. A blue thread-like river ran between rocky banks out into an open valley, and there, glinting in the sun, were eight little lakes like so many clear round mirrors. These must be the eight pools of which the stag had spoken.

They were farther away than they looked and it took Chang Py-ong half a day of difficult walking to reach the most distant one. The late afternoon sun blazed down upon the quiet surface as he stood beside it, the shadows of tall trees lay upon the white beach that bordered it, and a little way from the edge of the water grew bushes and an occasional pine. The lad found himself a hiding place easily enough and waited.

Before long he heard a soft silken sound as of great wings folding and there before him at the edge of the pool stood a dozen of the most beautiful creatures he had ever seen. They were tall and their high white feathery wings made them look taller than mortal maids. But when they had taken these off, folded them and laid them neatly over low branches of trees, they seemed like young girls just growing into womanhood. Their long black hair hung loose about their shoulders, their almond-shaped eyes were black and sparkling, their skin as clear and pale and lovely as ivory. How they laughed and romped together as they ran into the pool, splashing and tumbling, churning the quiet water into little waves and foaming bubbles! The shimmering stuff of which their garments were made seemed to shed the water like stiff silk and yet it was as soft and iridescent as mist.

Chang Py-ong watched, enchanted, forgetting what he had been told to do next. The sun dropped lower in the sky, the laughing, chattering damsels grew quieter. One by one they left the water and sat upon the beach together. Then the youth came to himself with a start. There was no time to lose, for undoubtedly the spirit-maids would be reclaiming their wings at any minute and flying back to the Other World. Quickly and silently he slipped from his hiding place, ran to the spot where the fairest of all the damsels had left her wings, seized them and carried them off.

None too soon. Almost at once the girls rose up from the beach, took again their wings, donned them and, one by one, flew off into the blue. At last they were all gone save the one whose wings Chang Py-ong held securely under his arm.

Pitifully the lovely creature made moan, running about from one tree to another looking for her lost wings. At last she sank down upon the shore and put her head in her hands disconsolately.

"Very selfish and thoughtless of her sister spirits to run off and leave her like that!" sputtered Chang Py-ong indignantly to himself.

Then he went up to the damsel and put his hand gently on

her shoulder. She started, looking up at him with terror. Chang Py-ong sat down beside her. His smile was friendly and reassuring. His heart was already filled with affection for the beautiful, unhappy maid, and love and pity prompted him to say tender things that quieted her fear. Soon she was smiling back at him and before the sun had set she had agreed willingly to follow him to his house at the foot of the mountain, marry him and live with him there as his contented and devoted wife.

In spite of the fast falling twilight the way back to Py-ong's home did not seem nearly so long and so difficult as the way out. They had much to talk about, these two, or rather Chang Py-ong had his whole life to relate and the girl listened, smiling and attentive. She did not talk very much in her turn, for how could a being from that strange far Other World explain to human ears about the life of spirit? At any rate they moved along with quick unhesitating steps and, in a remarkably short time, reached the walled garden of Chang Py-ong's home.

The sound of laughter and friendly talk drifted to their ears and, as they passed through the gate into the court between the two wings of the house where the household would have gathered, if there had been any household, they saw a goodly company waiting to greet them. Py-ong's servant, knowing by some strange means that his master would be wanting a marriage feast and guests to partake of it, had assembled all in readiness, both food and people.

So Chang Py-ong and the spirit-damsel were wedded, and they settled down into peaceful and uneventful living. They loved each other, they had enough of this world's goods for careful, simple living, and all went along as it should in happiness and prosperity.

In due time a girl child was born to them, as beautiful of face and gentle of manner as her mother. After the two had become accustomed to a third within the bonds of their love, Chang Py-ong noticed that his wife had grown unusually silent and sad.

"What is it, my love?" said he tenderly. "I cannot bear to see you thus sorrowful and distressed. Is there aught that I can do for you to bring back the happy laughter to your eyes and content again to your heart?"

Then the lady replied, looking imploringly into her husband's face, "Truly I am happy in my love for you, my dear one, and in our child. One thing only fills me with longing day and night. I want to go back to the land from which I came, to see once more my home and the sisters with whom I played. Even to see again my tall white feathery wings, and so remind myself that I am not of this world but of another, would bring me joy."

Her words pulled at Chang Py-ong's heart strings and he was tempted mightily to take out those wings from their hiding place and give them into his wife's keeping. Surely she loved him enough by now not to take advantage of them and fly away. But he remembered the warning of the stag and said nothing about the matter.

In time the lady grew contented again, and in the course of two years another child was born to them, a boy, handsome as his father, strong and merry. It is not customary in a

Korean family for the father to pay much attention to his small sons and daughters. Perhaps people would think a man proud if he showed affection or approval too plainly. But Chang Py-ong discarded such notions and played with his children, keeping them much at his side and showing openly his love for them.

Once again his wife grew sad and disconsolate, declaring that the one desire of her heart was to look upon her wings again, even if she could never place them on her shoulders. They were all that she would ever see that linked her to her old home. And again Chang Py-ong hardened his heart and kept the wings safely locked away.

When the third child came, he seemed more beautiful and lovable than even the other two. The family drew closer together and felt more united than ever before. But again the mood of depression fell upon the mother, and day and night she entreated her husband to let her but once see her shining wings and she would be satisfied.

Chang Py-ong began to waver. The stag had told him not to allow the lady to look at her spirit-wings until she had borne him four children. Well, were not three enough? Surely one woman could not carry off three all at once? And, anyway, she did not want to fly away, only to see the wings again. He was sure of that.

So, after many trying scenes in which his homesick wife begged and entreated him to show her the wings, he at last got them out. Taking them into the courtyard where she was sitting with their three children, he showed them to her.

"Let me put them upon my shoulders!" she cried, clapping

her hands with delight at the sight of them. "If I can feel their soft whiteness about me I shall know again that I am spirit-born and not of this sad earth at all."

Chang Py-ong gently laid the tall pointed wings upon his wife's shoulders. There was a flash of light, a whir and flurry of feathers, an upswing of air, and there she was, high above him, with a child under each arm and one upon her back! He shaded his eyes and gazed longingly, mutely, until they vanished from his sight.

Bitterly did the young man grieve. Day after day, week after week, and finally month after month he moped disconsolately about his house. He could not forgive himself for having disregarded the warning of the stag, but, strangely enough, he did not blame his wife even in his heart for having deserted him and taken their children with her. Was she not spirit-born? How could he have expected to hold such a one chained by his love to this world? But he missed her; he longed for her and his three little ones with a hunger that could not be satisfied.

At length he decided to try again to find the eight mirror-like lakes. Might it not be possible that his wife would fly to earth with her sister spirits to sport and bathe in the eighth pool as she used to do? If he could only see her he might persuade her to come back to him, that they might live out their lives together until the time came for him to die.

One early dawn he set out, found the trail without too much difficulty and, in due time, stood on the white beach beside the clear quiet water of the eighth pool.

There was no sign of life in or around it and, after gazing

sadly at its lonely unbroken surface, he turned to find himself a hiding place as he had done before. Directly behind him stood the stag, though he had heard no step, no breaking of twig or any sound of his approach. They stared at each other for a moment in silence. Was it scorn or laughter that glinted in the creature's eyes?

"So you have come back seeking the lady," said the stag. "But you will not see her. Since the day you carried her away to be your wife the spirits have ceased to visit this pool."

"Is there no place where I can find her?" cried Chang Py-ong desperately. "Truly life is worth nothing to me without her. Rather would I leave this earth myself forever than to go on from day to day in loneliness without her and my three little ones!"

"Do you mean that?" said the stag.

"I do in very truth."

"Well then, the matter is simple. Go you to the seventh pool which lies to the east of this one not more than an hour's walking. When twilight dims the bright mountain air you will see a large bucket let down from the darkening sky by a long strong cable of rope. That will be the servants of the lords of the Other World drawing up water, for these magic pools have sweeter water from their eternal springs than any other in all the universe. Waste no time but swim out and climb aboard the bucket. Then you will be pulled up into the realm of spirits. Doubtless your wife will be waiting for you with joy in her eyes."

The sound of the stag's voice had grown silken and monotonous and an overpowering desire to sleep fell upon Chang

Py-ong. He closed his eyes for a moment, and when he opened them again the creature had vanished and twilight had already deepened the shadows of the woods round about.

He pulled himself together and set off at a jog-trot run in the direction of the seventh pool. When he reached it he could just distinguish in the graying light the outline of a large bucket at the end of a rope, apparently suspended from nothing at all far up in the sky. He plunged into the water, then swam with all speed and seized the rim of it just as it dipped below the surface. Climbing into the bucket was a difficult matter, but, kicking and scrambling, he managed to, and scarcely had he tumbled into the bottom when it began to rise.

Chang Py-ong grinned to himself. "It's likely their spirit-lordships will find themselves low in drinking water! Evidently the pullers-up have mistaken my weight for what they were after and will be surprised!"

Up and up he sped. Clouds surrounded him, sailed under him. Stars came out in the darkening sky so near he could almost touch them. Up and up and up and up . . . . Suddenly he saw a dawn-lighted shore. The bucket swung closer, and there stood his wife waving to him, calling to him, and the three little ones reaching out their arms to him. His heart sang with joy as the bucket bumped against the glistening sand. He leaped out and clasped them in his arms, then followed them across the fields, deep into the spirit world.

No one in his village at the foot of the haunted mountain ever saw or heard of Chang Py-ong again. But a hunter once told a strange tale of adventure in the wood nearby. He had got lost, he said, and wandered farther into the mountains than he realized. Suddenly he came upon a stag, beautiful, with antlered head raised high. He lifted his weapon to slay him but, looking into his large brown eyes, he could not find it in his heart to kill the creature. His arm dropped and the two stood gazing at each other for a long moment. Then the stag spoke.

"I thank you for your impulse of kindness," he said. "Now go your way and leave me to mine. You will see the trail if you watch closely—the trail that leads to Chang Py-ong's house. He will not use it again for he is happy, very happy— elsewhere."

13. THE VALLEY
OF TEN THOUSAND WATERFALLS

IN THE Diamond Mountains there are many Buddhist
shrines and monasteries, great silence and tranquillity on

snowy peaks, and in the valleys the sound of many waters. Especially in Man-pog-dong, the Vale of Ten Thousand Waterfalls, the rush and tumble of falling streams is never absent and in spring floods the roar of them fills the ears every waking moment and troubles the dreams of the sleeper.

There was once, in the old days, a lad named To-jong who lived in the valley beside one of the ten thousand waterfalls for which it was named. He was a quiet, thoughtful lad and liked to wander by himself along the stream or into the deep woods and up the steep sides of the mountains. His father and mother let him go where he would and never worried about him. He had a good head on his shoulders and always seemed to know what to do in any small emergency which the family had to meet. And there were plenty of those for it was a large family and small brothers and sisters were always getting into difficulties, to say nothing of calamities that befell the chickens, the goats, the ox team and the stubborn stupid donkey, for To-jong's father farmed a small plot of land. The boy had a way with him, especially with children and animals. In his hands was a healing touch and his gentle quiet soothed troubled minds, banished fears and shed about him an air of contentment and well-being. Not that he said much. He was a curiously silent person.

Though his parents were ignorant, somehow or other To-jong had picked up a knowledge of reading and he was forever writing verses on bits of bark or walking miles to the home of the nearest yangban who allowed him to borrow books of the poets. The boy loved quiet, and that was hard to come by in his big noisy family. He sometimes even wished he might get away from the roar of the nearby waterfall and the scrambling rush of the stream hurrying past his home and down through the valley. His mind was always full of wonderful thoughts that he wanted to listen to and mull over carefully.

One day, in early summer when he had done his share of the work around the little farm, he asked his mother for a bit of food—some cucumbers especially. These he put in a purse-bag which he tied to his waist, then started out, saying he would not be back for a few days. He was going high up into the mountains, he said. He intended to lie out under the stars at night and wander through the great forests by day. What he wanted most of all, though he did not say so, was to go beyond the sound of the falling water in the glen and be for a little while where there was utter stillness.

He climbed out of the Valley of Ten Thousand Waterfalls, crossed a range and followed an almost hidden trail up and over a high peak of the Diamond Mountains, and then descended to a green and lovely plateau. The sound of rushing water had long been left behind him, there was no wind and a deep silence hung over the motionless trees scattered over the upland meadow through which he now walked, slowly and in great content. Even his footsteps fell soundlessly on the soft springy earth.

To-jong was as happy as a bird. He loved the feel of the warm sun on his back, the unbroken blue of the sky overhead and the gentleness of the landscape around him. He would write a poem about it all soon, but now he was so intent on just feeling and being that words and even thoughts seemed unnecessary. After a while his soaring spirit was brought down to earth by the realization that he was hungry and dreadfully thirsty. He looked about him with a more critical eye and stood still to listen. There was no spot in his home valley where he could not catch the sound of tumbling water. But here the unbroken silence told him no mountain stream ran nearby where he might drink. Well, a cucumber would be refreshing and perhaps satisfy his thirst. He sat down where he was and made a scanty meal, keeping more than half of his supply of food for future use. He had not the least idea how far he had come or how long it would take him to reach home, when he was ready to return, which he was not, as yet. And he was still thirsty. For a moment the thought of the sound of falling waters seemed good to him. He got up from the shady spot under a tree where he had been sitting and wandered on.

The plateau flattened out more and more. Bald patches of rock cropped out and the rank meadow grass fell away. To-jong looked about and listened. It seemed at length as if his ear caught a faint far splashing and rushing, as of a stream. He moved off in that direction and descended through a thickening forest of evergreens into a lush green valley. This is the place, he thought, where I shall find water, but even with the thinking he realized that the sound of it was no longer there. The air was as still as it had been on the plateau, unnaturally still, for no call or song of bird broke the silence of the tree tops, no rustle and stir of any little living creatures in the underbrush.

How long To-jong wandered around in that breathless

valley he could never have told. The trees opened out, the sun beat pitilessly down upon him, the mountains seemed to close about him in a menacing manner, and the thirst in him grew and grew until it was like a raging fever and it seemed as if he could bear it no longer.

He stood for a moment leaning against the bole of a great tree, his tongue parched and dry, his body wet with sweat, his eyes burning. He must find water, he *must!*

Suddenly he saw, not a hundred yards away, the glint of sunlight on a gleaming surface. With a cry of joy he rushed toward it. Water! A pool! Yes, there was no mistaking it! Willow trees and then a little pond standing out in the open, mirroring the blue sky. As To-jong drew close to it he saw that someone had got there before him. Kneeling on the bank, her head bent over the still water as if gazing at herself in it, was the slender figure of a girl in blue silk cut in the fashion of a long-ago Chinese dynasty. The boy hesitated, expecting her to turn her head at his approach, but she remained as still and unmoving as a statue. To-jong stepped closer; he felt a sudden keen desire to look into her face. Still she did not move even when he stood right behind her. He peered over her shoulder into the clear pool below and then uttered a cry of astonishment. There was no reflection of her whatever. The water lay unruffled, blue as the sky above it; the image of trees and leaves along its edge was clear and unbroken, with no girl's face looking back at its original. His own form and face were mirrored, quite alone. He glanced again toward the blue-clad figure of the girl at his feet, and it was gone, vanished as if melted into the air. To-jong ran first in one direction, then in another, unable to believe that the damsel could have disappeared completely, leaving no trace behind her.

He must have become confused for he could not find the pool again. It was gone as surely as the girl. Could he have imagined the whole thing? No, he told himself, he could not. It had been real, actual. What was more, his thirst was still upon him, greater than ever. His ears rang, the sun burned fiercely upon him, and he thought if he could not find water soon to ease his parched mouth and throat he would go mad.

For an hour or two To-jong wandered again, scarcely knowing what he was about except that he listened always for the sound of running water. And again he heard it, a small silken trickling as of a stream purling over a pebbly bed. He followed it and once again he caught a gleam of sunlight falling on a pool. He hurried toward it, and there stood the girl in blue, her black hair undone and hanging over her shoulders.

This time the thirst was so fierce in him that he stayed not to see whether she cast a reflection like an ordinary mortal or did not. He fell upon his face on the bank of the still water and drank and drank. It was cold and pure; never, To-jong thought, had he tasted anything so sweet and good. When he had drunk his fill he turned toward the girl—or rather where she had been, for she was no longer there. In her stead was a blue pigeon with soft, iridescent neck, very beautiful. It walked about fearlessly near him, pecking at invisible morsels of food on the ground. Then it spread its wings and flew up into the branches of a nearby tree.

To-jong watched it, enchanted. It would fly off a little way and then stop, waiting until he followed. On and on they went, the lovely blue creature fluttering from tree to tree, the boy coming after. At long last they reached a cave in the side of the mountain, and To-jong peered in curiously. Inside lay a thick book covered with dust and blown leaves, and an antique incense burner. When he looked for the blue pigeon again it had vanished. A sudden weariness overcame him and he could scarcely drag himself into the shelter of the cave and lie down before he was asleep.

His dreams were troubled and so vivid that he seemed to to be seeing with his outward eye and hearing with his outward ear. A soft light filled the cave and he saw the strange unearthly girl in blue leading in an old man in the yellow habit of a Buddhist monk. They stood looking down upon him for a moment, then the man spoke.

"My son, we have been at great pains to draw you hither, this damsel from the Heavenly Kingdom and I from the world of the dead. We ask of you a great gift. This cave where we stand was once the shrine and cell of a gentle soul, a hermit who, by his life of prayer and his great love for all living creatures, exerted power and influence such as you cannot imagine. Because of him the beasts of the forest grew friendly with one another, the birds unafraid, and pilgrims came from down in the valley to learn from him of God, to be healed in body and comforted in mind. His spirit has now gone beyond the wheel of births and deaths but the world has need of him. Will you, my son, give your life to take his place?"

It seemed to To-jong as if he answered simply, "For that was I born into this world. I know now. But tell me, brother, how I may go about this task. How can I learn the truths which that holy hermit knew? How can I live a life of prayer and love and become as he was?"

The old man stooped and picked up the volume lying on the floor of the cave. "This book contains the teachings of the Lord Buddha," he said. "He knew the way. Learn of him."

Days passed in the Valley of Ten Thousand Waterfalls. To-jong's father and mother and all his little brothers and sisters watched anxiously for his return. Week followed week and month followed month and then the years went by. His family grieved for him, believing at length that he must have been killed by a tiger. His mother wept night after night until time softened the pain in her heart and To-jung became to her only a sweet and sad memory.

After many years rumors began to run through the small villages in the valley, meeting other similar stories of travelers from the outside world. People said there was a strange hermit who dwelt in the heart of the Diamond Mountains. He was a very holy man indeed. He sheltered himself from the cold and storms of winter in a cave. There was no need of shelter from the wild beasts of the forests for they were gentle and friendly with him and with one another whenever he was near.

"I was lost for days," said a traveler, "and had given myself up for dead. As I lay exhausted and dying on a wild mountainside there came a man in the yellow robe of a Buddhist monk. He lifted me up on his shoulders as easily as if I had been a child and carried me into his cave. There he fed and nursed me till my strength had returned and then set me on the trail that led me home. I have been a different man ever since."

"I too found the hermit's cave," said another. "He was sitting outside it in a patch of sunlight. A tiger lay asleep at his feet, wildcats climbed quietly in the trees nearby and birds rested on his shoulders and fed from his hands. It was very still there, no sound at all except the trickling of a little mountain stream. I have felt a great peace in my soul ever since he taught me to pray."

At first people happened upon the cave and the holy man by accident, but after a while, when tales of him had spread far and wide, they set out purposely to find him. Pilgrims of all kinds climbed up through the Valley of Ten Thousand Waterfalls until a trail was beaten through the forests. Up the mountainside it led, across the range and the upland meadows, down into the hidden glen and up again on the other side, on and on until it stopped at the mouth of the cave. Inside they could see only a thick book, an ancient incense burner and the few necessities a hermit might need. Usually they found him outside waiting for them, as if he expected them. They called him the Master and it never occurred to anyone that he was the same gentle thoughtful boy To-jong, who had wandered into the mountains so long ago and never returned.

Quiet he was, now as always, with a kind of listening, waiting quiet. His face held peace in it and love, his hands had a healing touch. Many brought their troubles to him. After he had heard them he kept very still for a few moments, then he would smile gently and speak the words of advice or comfort that the anxious ones most needed. Sometimes his strong kind hands, laid upon a sick or hurt child, brought relief and then well-being.

People went to him, not he to them. Always he was to be found in his cave or walking about or sitting right outside of it among the beasts and birds. But there came a day when the cave was empty and the friendly forest creatures looked in vain for the Master To-jong. He had arisen with the sun and with a faintly troubled look in his calm and always happy face he had taken the trail that led to the Valley of Ten Thousand Waterfalls. It was a warm spring day, the snow on the mountainsides was melting fast. Only on the high peaks and in little cold clefts of the hills where the sun could not penetrate did it still lie white and drifted.

To-jong strode along. He who had been born where the sound of falling waterfalls was never out of his hearing knew the language in which they spoke. He had listened to the one small trickling stream near his cave and knew; he had caught a warning note, a terrible prediction. Up over the mountain so lovely in the new green of spring he walked with quick step, down to the lush warm intervale where he had once caught the gleam of sunlight on clear magic pools and seen for a moment a blue-clad damsel from another world; over the rocky plateau and down at last to the Valley of Ten Thousand Waterfalls. For only a moment he stopped to embrace his mother and summon the rest of his family.

"Come! Come quickly!" he said. "Gather all the people of the village together—and those from other towns and farms —all who live where the land is low or beside streams and waterfalls. Let those who are strong carry the old and the weak and the little children. Bid them come at once to the market place."

So insistent were his words, with such authority did he speak, that no one hesitated for a moment to obey him. Soon a long line of frightened, puzzled people came streaming in from all the homes in the Valley of Ten Thousand Waterfalls. The market place where To-jong stood, directing, encouraging, hastening, became full. The holy man climbed upon a stone and addressed them. People strained their ears and could scarce hear what he said, though he shouted. The sound of many waters filled the air, the tumbling rush of swollen streams had become a roar. To-jong's voice was lost in the tumult of sound, but he waved his arms, gesticulated, urged them on. They understood. They moved at once up into the hills.

There was no panic, no confusion. Strong men carried the frail, farmers drove or led their beasts and fowls, children trotted along close to their mothers. After the whole valley had been cleared To-jong followed his people.

From high up on the mountainside they looked back at their valley homes. The flooded streams and thundering waterfalls were pouring into it. The floor of the valley became a lake which rose higher and higher, spreading out, muddy, tumultuous, frightening. To-jong took the lead, turning away from it, and the people straggled after him. Strangely enough no one seemed sad or anxious. They came at length to the upland plateau and rested.

"Not a bad place to start a new village, right here," said one.

"It's on the trail to *his* cave," said another.

"Yes," agreed several, looking toward To-jong. "We shall be nearer to him than we were in the Valley of Ten Thousand Waterfalls."

"Strange to think that such a holy man was once just one of us," someone added.

"But he always was quiet and thoughtful—odd, you might say."

To-jong's mother was standing nearby. She smiled happily as she glanced toward her son. "Not odd unless gentleness and love are odd," she said. "They call him a holy one and no doubt he is, but even being a holy one is not so very strange, is it? I have always known this about To-jong, and it does not seem odd to me—that where he is there will be quietness and friendliness and peace."

14. THREE WHO
FOUND THEIR HEARTS' DESIRE

THERE were once three brothers, Zong-Teg, the eldest,
Zong-Yong, the youngest, and Zong-Og, the middle one,
who was often called Second Son. They lived with their
father, who was an old man, feeble and almost helpless.
When their mother had been alive they were prosperous and
happy. Their home had been large, and warm in winter; they
had had many servants and chests of money to provide them
with comforts and luxuries. But after she died misfortune
soon fell upon the sorrowful widower and his three sons.
Sickness, failure of the rice paddies, one thing and then

another, made their wealth shrink and shrink until there was scarcely enough left to keep them from starving. The boys were still too young to find work that would bring in money when their father lost what strength he had and could do little of anything for them. He grieved daily that this should be so and sometimes said with a sigh, "Alas! Ai-goo! would that I were dead so that you, my sons, might be free to go out into the world and win your fortunes!"

They were good lads, the three of them, and loved their father truly, so they bade him never so to wish while they were alive to take care of him. And care for him they did, faithfully and tenderly. Zong-Teg gathered dead wood in the nearby ancient forest, and sold it in bundles of faggots, thereby earning enough to buy a little food. Zong-Yong helped wherever he could, and Zong-Og, whose hands were gentlest and whose heart perhaps was the most loving, tended their father when he became too ill and frail to do for himself, and kept the house and cooked the food almost as well as if he were a girl instead of the tall, strapping lad that he was.

The boys never complained even to each other but in their hearts they often wished their lives might be pleasanter and more full of fun and interest. It was dull and depressing for them just doing their humdrum daily duties. Zong-Teg could remember the old times when there had been good food, soft clothing, much laughter, the coming and going of many guests, and nothing required of him but play—and a little study—all the day long. Zong-Og remembered, too, but in his mind lingered most of all the thought of their gentle mother whose arms were always open to the three of them when anything went wrong, and who was always there, playing with them, telling them stories, loving them even when she had to scold them a little. Zong-Og thought she must have been the most beautiful and lovingest woman in all the world.

As for Zong-Yong, he was too little when their mother died and their prosperity and comfort left them to remember about it. Perhaps that was the reason, in part at least, that he was the most cheerful of the three, taking things as they were and managing somehow to enjoy life and make a good time for himself.

Sometimes, after their old father had gone to sleep in the early evening, the three would daydream together of what they would like to be and do "sometime" in the far future. They did not picture to themselves or each other the actual time when their father would die and they would be free to go out in the world and shift for themselves, but perhaps he himself had put the idea into their heads when he had spoken of seeking their fortune. At any rate it came to be a topic of conversation when the boys were alone and, for a short time at least, idle.

"Someday I would like to be a man of substance," Zong-Teg would say. "Money, gold—all that I might wish to spend on myself, and of course my family. Naturally I would marry and have many sons and daughters."

"Ho! who would want to be tied down to a house and family, even if one had strings and strings of cash!" Zong-Yong would reply. "*I* want to see the world—someday—and be very famous, known to everyone, even the king himself!"

Zong-Og usually smiled wistfully when the other two were thus building dream castles, and said nothing. One time his brothers pressed him for an answer.

"And what would you like to have and do, when we are all a lot older?" prodded Zong-Yong.

"Yes, tell us now, what is *your* heart's desire? Or maybe you haven't got any!" said Zong-Teg.

"What I want most in life, what I long to find, someday, is perhaps more impossible than what you wish for," replied Zong-Og, speaking slowly and thoughtfully. "Wealth and fame are all very well but they are not my heart's desire and would mean nothing to me without it."

"And what may that be?" questioned both brothers.

"A woman to be my wife who is as loving and gay and beautiful as our mother was."

In due time the old man reached the end of his feeble strength and knew that he was about to die. He called his three sons to him and said to them, "My children, I have nothing to leave you but my gratitude and the memory of my love. You have been good and faithful sons to me, and I wish that I had a fortune to divide between you. I have only three poor gifts, my dears, but life is strange and often generous to those who are loving and true, as you have been. These—even these poor bequests—may be the means of your finding happiness. Who can say?"

With that he bade Zong-Teg bring out the three objects that he had cherished carefully ever since the long-ago days of their prosperity. When these had been laid on the floor beside his sleeping mat, he pointed with a trembling finger.

"This ancient hand-mill," he said, "with its grinding stones, is old but still useful. This shall be yours, my First Born.

"And to you, my Second Son," he continued, looking with affection upon Zong-Og, "I give my smooth, worn bamboo walking stick and the half-gourd that we have used as a bowl these many years."

Then his thin shaking hands traveled gently over the form of an old-fashioned drum, long and with a narrow waist. He smiled feebly as he said, "Zong-Yong, you are ever wont to be merry. You have cheered my old heart often with your laughter and your singing. It is fitting that to you I leave the drum that gave me happy hours in my youth."

So their father died and the sons were sad for they loved him, but for his sake they rejoiced, because death meant release from weariness and helplessness and pain. They chose a tomb with great care and gave him reverent burial and, when all had been done as it should be, they started out into the world to seek their fortunes, each carrying the gift the dying father had left him.

For a while they traveled together, but when they came to an intersection of three roads they decided to separate, each taking one.

"We shall miss each other," said Zong-Teg, "but it will be good for us to take our chances alone. Fortune might be frightened and run away if she met three of us, all at once, and ready to make such heavy demands on her!"

Zong-Yong grinned. "Yes, fame for me! And a lot of it, so that I shall come to know even the king himself!"

"And gold for me—also lots of it!" Zong-Teg added merrily.

"And for me the fairest and most loving wife in the world!" Zong-Og had not changed his heart's desire any more than had his brothers.

So the three embraced each other and said farewell, yet were loath to part.

"In ten years let us meet again at this very spot," the eldest suggested. "And then we can compare our fortunes and decide which of us has the greatest cause for thankfulness."

The other two agreed at once and each took one of the three roads before him.

Zong-Teg had chosen the right-hand road. He traveled along at a brisk pace, carrying the old hand-mill first on one shoulder then on the other. It was heavy, and by sundown the boy felt he must stop and rest for the night. A strip of forest land lay on one side of him and he pushed his way through the underbrush until he came to a small clearing made by a huge, many-branched tree so thick with leaves that nothing would grow under it. This seemed like a snug and safe place to sleep so Zong-Teg made himself as comfortable as he could, leaning against the bole of the tree, and soon dozed off.

He awoke with a start to find himself in complete darkness. Night had fallen and the air was full of mysterious rustles and murmurings. A twig snapped nearby and the creaking of two boughs against each other made an eerie sound. Zong-Teg's pulse beat fast. He wished his two brothers had come along with him. He wished he had stayed on the road where there was probably at least a little thinning of the darkness. Then he heard something that made his heart leap right up into his throat; a brushing of some creature through the thick undergrowth that surrounded the big tree, steps crackling over dead leaves, and twigs, and muffled voices.

Quickly and silently as a cat the boy jumped up and climbed the tree against which he had been leaning. Almost without realizing it he carried the old mill up with him. When he had found a crotch to sit in he was glad that he had it. If he had left it on the ground whoever or whatever was coming nearer might have found it and perhaps looked for the owner. He sat very still, scarcely daring to breathe. He could see nothing whatever in the black darkness below him but he soon heard the voices of men. Evidently there were two of them.

"A fine haul we have made this night," said one.

"There!" said the other, breathing heavily and dumping something on the ground with a thud. "Enough gold and gems to make us rich for the rest of our lives!"

"And no danger whatever of being caught," said the first voice. "We have robbed the king of thieves himself—and he knows nothing of it!"

"Nor would he dare to pursue us with the law," said the second voice, chuckling. "Things would then become too hot for him."

"We can rest here for the present." The first man yawned

noisily as he spoke. "No human being will be about in this thick woods at midnight."

The two rustled around for a few moments more, then there was silence, soon broken by snores.

Zong-Teg moved his cramped legs cautiously. His knee knocked against the handle of the clumsy mill and it let forth an odd rattling sound. The boy held his breath in terror but the snoring tunes from below continued unbroken. He would climb down, he thought, and get away. Then he hesitated. How could he possibly escape in the pitch-dark and through the noisy underbrush without rousing those two robbers below him? And he had no idea where they were lying. He might even drop right on top of them as he let go of the branch he was sitting on. Better stay where he was and take a chance of their not seeing him in the morning. He moved the hand-mill into a more secure position. It rattled again. Suddenly he had a thought! Seizing the handle, he turned it vigorously. The rough stones ground together with a grating, thunderous sound, for all the world like a strange beast snarling in the darkness.

The snores from below stopped abruptly. With screams of terror the two robbers leaped up and plunged into the underbrush. Zong-Teg could hear them cursing, shouting to each other, crashing through tangled vines, howling with fear and the pain of scratched arms and faces. Then the sounds grew fainter and more distant and at last there was silence.

The boy stayed where he was until the first gray streaks of daylight. Then he climbed stiffly down and examined the chest that the robbers had left behind them. It was fair-sized but not too large to carry, and it was full to the brim of gold pieces and jewels—rubies, emeralds, diamonds and other precious and semi-precious stones, enough for a king's ransom. The rope that had fastened the chest shut and the wicker crate, or jiggy, by which it had been carried lay near at hand. Zong-Teg adjusted the rope and swung the jiggy to his shoulders. He left the hand-mill where the chest had been.

"Farewell, gift of my father," said he, addressing it with a bow. "I wish I could take you with me, but I have all that I can carry. You have already accomplished more than he could have dreamed. You have won me my heart's desire!"

Now Zong-Yong had taken the left-hand road where the three had intersected. He had hung the narrow-waisted old drum from his shoulders, and as he tramped along he beat a merry tune upon it, breaking forth into a song of his own composing:

> "*Rat*-a-tat-*tat*-a-tat-tan,
>   Was there ever a luckier man?
>   With a good drum to beat,
>   I've the world at my feet,
>   And a fortune to find where I can!
>   A-*rat*-a-tat-tat,
>   A-*rat*-a-tat-tat,
>   I'm a most un-pre-dict-able man!"

He hummed and drummed and stepped along jauntily, savoring the word *unpredictable,* rolling it around on his tongue. He was not quite sure what it meant but it had a rather exciting sound and just the right beat. He tried another stanza:

> "*Rat*-a-tat-*tat*-a-tat-tan,
>   I've neither a goal nor a plan,
>   But adventure will come
>   To the roll of my drum,
>   And I'll meet it the best that I can!
>   A-*rat*-a-tat-tat,
>   A-*rat*-a-tat-tat,
>   I'm a most un-pre-dict——"

Zong-Yong stopped short in the middle of his favorite word and in the midst of a drum beat. A most unpredictable thing was happening right then and there under his very nose! Out of the woods to his right had jumped a large yellow tiger. He crouched in the road not three yards behind the terrified boy, weaving his great head from side to side, his green eyes glittering. Zong-Yong was too paralyzed with fright to stir, expecting the beast to spring at him and devour him before he could take another breath. But the tiger did no such thing. He only continued to move his head from side to side, rhythmically, monotonously, keeping the rest of his body taut and motionless.

A thought sprang into Zong-Yong's mind and he began a gentle rat-a-tat-tat on his drum, stepping slowly backward away from the crouching animal. The tiger got up at once and, keeping perfect time, marched after him. The boy drummed a quicker, louder rhythm and the beast began to dance as lightly and gracefully on his huge clawed paws as a kitten. Zong-Yong varied the beat of his drum and the creature moved accordingly, now slow, now fast and faster. But always his step was soft and light, the rhythmic swinging of his powerful body beautiful.

Thus they continued down the long road, the boy becoming more confident, yet not daring to turn his back to the tiger and move face forward. The animal kept a distance of two or three yards behind him.

They came at length to a village. Men, women and children fled screaming at sight of them, then crept back out of their houses and from corners and sheltering places to watch the strange sight. At the center of the market place Zong-Yong gave out and sank to the ground exhausted. Now, he thought to himself, now I can drum no more and the spell will be broken!

Not at all! The tiger sprawled beside him, regarded him in not unfriendly fashion and rested his great head upon his paws. The villagers drew cautiously nearer.

"A trick beast?" asked one.

"Very clever and well trained," remarked another.

"Remarkably tame!" said a third.

Whereupon a child, bolder than the rest, ran to the tiger and buried its hands in the soft striped fur. The animal twitched his ears a little, looked at the child with a bored expression, then paid no further attention.

Thoughts were gathering in Zong-Yong's mind. "Yes, oh yes," he said, "very clever, this tiger of mine, and as gentle as a kitten." He took off his hat and began to circulate it among the increasing crowd. "Any small coin would be welcome," said he, bowing right and left, "or—if it should so happen that any of you have food to spare—it is a long time since either of us has eaten!"

The people of the village outdid themselves. They feasted Zong-Yong and the tiger till they were full to bursting. The most important man among them invited the boy to stay at his house, and the animal had an admiring circle watching him whenever he ate. He seemed quite indifferent to them, and dozed contentedly in the market place.

Before he left the town the next day Zong-Yong gave a special performance. He drummed tunes of all kinds, marching, dancing, soft, loud, merry, slow, and to every tune the tiger danced, treading lightly on his great paws, swaying his body, swinging his noble, powerful head, always in perfect time. People were beside themselves with delight. Never had they seen anything so wonderful! They accompanied the two out of town and halfway to the next village.

Now to make a long story short, the fame of Zong-Yong and his wonder beast flew before them and grew like a snowball rolling down hill. In every town they drew bigger crowds than in the last; in no time at all they were known about, then expected, then invited hither and yon by special messengers. And finally they were commanded to appear in the royal palace before the king himself.

His Majesty was so enchanted that he made Zong-Yong one of his ministers and the tiger a royal pet. Both lived thereafter in comfort and luxury and were much waited on. Before ten years had passed Zong-Yong had married a princess, quite forgetting he never intended to be tied down, and had become famous throughout Seoul and all the country round about.

Sometimes he wondered how it had all happened. Perhaps the tiger, Gesong, as he had named him, had once belonged to a band of public entertainers, had been tamed and trained by them and had escaped. In a way it was Gesong who had made him his fame and his fortune, but before the tiger it was his father's legacy of the ancient, narrow-waisted drum to which he was beholden, which had won for him his heart's desire.

The second son, Zong-Og, had taken the middle road, as was fitting and proper. He carried his father's bamboo walking stick, smooth as ivory, and under his arm the old bowl made out of half a gourd and satiny to the touch. He walked with a leisurely step, for he liked to savor the beauty of the landscape. Mountains rose in front of him, their snow-topped peaks glittering in the sun, and on either side stretched forests green and rustling and sweet-smelling. And when the woods thinned out there were fields thick with wild flowers, a riot of color and alive with bees and little birds. The road ran downhill into a valley which apparently separated him from the distant mountains, and as he continued he came upon rice paddies with workers busy in them, their heads sheltered from the sun by broad-brimmed hats. Zong-Og had a happy smile on his face and he loitered on his way, filling his lungs with the soft sweet air and his heart with pleasure at the lovely sights and sounds all about him. There was no need to hurry.

Suddenly he realized that twilight had come upon him.

The distant hills changed from white to pink, then crimson and mauve, and finally disappeared into the fast-growing dark. He quickened his steps. Doubtless there was a village nearby, for he had met occasional walkers on the road and once or twice a donkey almost hidden by the heavily laden baskets hanging down on each side of him. But now the road was empty; not a soul in sight and no sign of human habitation. Curious how quickly the night folded down and hid things away. It made walking along a strange way difficult. Zong-Og had not felt tired before. Now his legs were so weary he thought he must lie down somewhere and rest until daylight.

He left the road, stepping into what he thought was an open field, but he soon discovered it was full of obstacles. A little stumbling around, feeling cautiously and straining his eyes to make out dim outlines, convinced him that he was in a graveyard. He hesitated, a superstitious fear prickling his skin, then he shrugged his shoulders, laughed a little shakily and said aloud to himself, "Well, what of it? Why should a strong boy be afraid of either ghosts or takgabbis?" (Those are the mischievous goblins who like to play practical jokes and frighten people. Often they work real harm, for their power is great.)

With that he felt about until he had found a tomb of some size and lay down close beside it, placing his gourd bowl and his bamboo stick where he could put his hands on them. They gave him a sense of home and friendliness, and he soon fell asleep.

He was wakened by a sharp sound as of a stick striking

the tomb just above his head. He lay still, trembling in the black dark. It came again, followed by a whispery voice scarcely distinguishable from the wind in the leaves of nearby trees.

"Get up, old bones," it rustled. "Come along with me. I have work for you to do, merry work, *charming* work!" There followed cackling laughter, mirthless, uncanny.

Zong-Og scarcely breathed. Then the stick beat upon the tombstone again angrily. "Stop cowering and hiding, old crack-boned skeleton! Come up out of the moldy ground! Come up! Answer me!"

Zong-Og, shaking with terror, clung to the tomb, trying to hide behind it, forgetting that in the thick darkness no one could see him no matter where he stood. No one? Not even a takgabbi?

"Answer me," the voice repeated, "or I'll grind to powder whatever bones are left you!"

Still the boy said nothing. In a moment the whispers continued. "We are walking together tonight, you and I, into the city. Come up! Hold out an arm that I may feel you. I can't see you, you know."

At that hope leaped into Zong-Og's frightened heart. The creature, whatever it was, could not see in the dark. If he could only follow it back to the road he might escape.

"I'm coming, Sir," he whispered back, and the fear still in him made his teeth chatter.

There was a long pause. Then the voice said, "You don't sound quite dead. Unless you are a skeleton, you won't do. Let me feel you."

Tremblingly Zong-Og reached out his satin-smooth gourd, bottom up, in the direction of the voice. Something touched and felt of it.

Again the cackling laughter. "Skeleton, true enough! And old—old! That is your skull, I suppose. Hold out your arm that I may take it and we may go together."

Zong-Og pushed the bamboo stick forward and the creature grasped it. "By all the tricks of the takgabbis, you must have died of starvation, your bones are so thin!" it cried.

Keeping his hand on the other end of the stick, the boy suddenly felt himself lifted into the air. The night wind rushed by his face, his legs seemed to stream out behind him like a heron's. The stars overhead hung closer and there was a sense of lightness and exhilaration through all his body. It would have been fun if he had not been so breathless and so fearful of what might happen next.

In a very short time he became conscious of dropping slowly and easily through the air and then dragging his toes ever so gently along the ground. Then he was walking on it, solidly and firmly. Lights shone not very far away, evidently from a city toward which his steps were directed.

Now, thought Zong-Og, my end is surely near. Just as soon as a light falls upon us my takgabbi (for he was sure by this time that his companion was such a one) will see that I am not a skeleton at all but a very much alive boy! He thought of letting go the stick and running off—anywhere. But how could he expect to escape the magic power of a takgabbi? Moreover he was very curious as to what this strange adventure might lead to, so he walked on in silence. Fortunately for him they had no sooner entered the gate of the city than the little lights they had seen went out, one by one. It must be past midnight, thought Zong-Og, and all the world is in bed and going to sleep.

They turned from the road and entered a garden. The boy was sure of that because of the smell of growing things and the occasional dim outline of shrubs and then of a house. How the goblin managed to pass through doors and into rooms, dragging him along, Zong-Og could not imagine. At length they stood before a heavy paper partition through which shone a very faint glow as from a small lamp turned down low. The takgabbi had dropped its end of the bamboo stick and Zong-Og cowered back into a corner filled with blacker shadows. But apparently the goblin was now too intent upon business to take notice of the supposed skeleton, and, except close to the partition, it was too dark to see, anyway.

"Behind this door," it whispered, "lies a young girl, very sick. I am minded to steal her soul away and make merry with it among my companions. But only if a hand of death is laid upon her and her soul is borne first to an abode of death can I accomplish what I wish. Hence your company, friend skeleton. Now, heed well what I am saying. Take this bag." Something was thrown into the dark, and Zong-Og caught a silky-feeling substance in his hand. "Go into that room," the creature continued, "hold the bag under the nostrils of the girl on the sleeping mat, and I will make the proper spells and incantations. When you have caught her breath in the bag, bring it to me. Then her soul will be mine."

Zong-Og felt like saying, "I will do no such thing!" then letting out a scream that would wake the household, but he swiftly swallowed the scream and blocked the impulse. There was no telling what a takgabbi might do if it were angered, especially in the dark hours of the night when its powers were strongest. Better go on playing the game and perhaps he might find some way of protecting the poor sick girl from losing her soul.

Clutching the bag, he squeezed through the door and closed it quickly behind him, so that the light from the dim little lamp would not betray him. Over in a corner he saw a thick, rich-looking sleeping mat with a slight, motionless form lying on it. Carefully keeping himself from getting between the light and the partition beyond which the goblin was standing and might see his shadow, Zong-Og tiptoed over and gazed down at the sleeping girl. He caught his breath and a great surge of pity flooded through him. Such a thin, pale face, such a small, delicate, childlike body scarcely big enough to raise the level of the covers on the mat! Sick and in such grievous danger!

While he stood looking down at her the young maid opened her eyes. At first wonder filled them, then fear.

"Don't be frightened, my dear," Zong-Og hastened to reassure her in a low whisper. "I am here to protect you, not to harm you. Indeed I am sure now that Heaven has led me here to meet your destiny and mine this night." He knelt beside her, knowing in his heart that what he said was true.

The girl smiled at him, then closed her eyes again and went

to sleep. Yes, he knew that hers was the face he had dreamed of and this was the girl he would love to the end of his days. She would be his wife, his darling, his heart's desire.

Meanwhile a tremendous commotion was going on outside the room. The whole house shook, the air vibrated. Strange spells and incantations flew about as the whispery voice of the takgabbi rustled and muttered and hissed. Then suddenly everything stopped and quieted down for a moment, followed by a rush of stinging words.

"What are you doing, you worthless skeleton? Don't you know it is almost dawn? Hold the bag to her nose, let her breathe her soul into it! Quick! Quick! I can't do *everything* myself!"

Zong-Og smothered a giggle. He was not in the least afraid now. "Sorry," he whispered as loudly as he dared. "I'm new to this sort of thing, you know. Turn on your magic again and I'll get it."

Once more the air rumbled, the house shook and the takgabbi whispered and sputtered. Zong-Og took the bag from under his arm and blew into it until it was round and bulgy, then tied the strings around the neck of it, keeping the air in. "Perhaps I am breathing my own soul away," he said to himself, "but what matter? A soul lost for another is surely a soul won."

He slipped carefully out of the door again and in the darkness of the room outside held out the bag for the takgabbi to take. In a moment the creature had hold of it and was feeling it critically.

"Ah," it whispered with satisfaction, then handed the bag

back. "Now come! You must hold it till we get to your tomb
again where I can work my final magic. Give me your arm,
skeleton, but hurry! Morning is nearly upon us."

Zong-Og had moved into the darkest corner of the room.
He uttered an exclamation, then cried out, "Ai-goo! Sir, I
have dropped the bag. Shall we feel for it on the floor?"

The goblin hissed and rustled venomously but there was
nothing for it but to grope painfully around on the ground
while the boy gleefully held the bag high out of reach.

Finally the takgabbi stumbled over the bamboo stick and
screamed in fury. In the very midst of his rage a cock crowed
out in the yard and there was immediate and complete
silence.

Zong-Og stood where he was, not daring to move until
the gray dawn crept into the room. He found himself alone,
the takgabbi had vanished, but from somewhere in the depths
of the house there came sounds as of people stirring. He let
the air out of the bag he was holding, wondering for a moment whether he felt any different, whether his soul might
have slipped out of his body. But he felt exactly as usual, only
a little excited and very happy—and perhaps the least bit
noble! He would explain everything to the girl's father, she
would soon get well and they would be married! He climbed
quickly and silently over the high doorstep of the room,
found his way out to the veranda, and there sat down to await
further developments.

Ten years later the brothers met at the place they had
agreed upon. They greeted each other with great affection

for not once during that period had any one of the three set eyes upon another.

Zong-Teg came in a handsome sedan borne by liveried servants. He was clothed in costly white silk and rings glittered on his fingers and the elaborate hat of the yangban, or nobleman, was on his head. His voice boomed out heartily as he told of his adventures. "It is easy to see that I have won *my* heart's desire," he declared complacently. "I have everything that money can buy!"

Zong-Og wondered a little as he noted lines of discontent settling about the corners of his brother's mouth as soon as he stopped speaking.

Zong-Yong was heard and seen coming while still far down the road. Though he had left his pet tiger asleep in the palace yard, his brilliant-colored clothes and wide hat proclaimed him a showman, and he beat merrily upon his old narrow-waisted drum as he walked along, followed by a crowd of admiring small boys.

"Fame!" said he. "Ha! I am known and sought after through the length and breadth of Korea. Everybody knows me and Gesong, my tiger! I can go anywhere and do anything I like! Why, even the king—"

"So you have won *your* heart's desire also," interrupted Zong-Og. "Are you happy? Are you quite satisfied?"

Zong-Yong lifted his shoulders in a significant gesture. "Of course—naturally!" said he and he turned away, not meeting his brother's eyes. Zong-Og wondered.

Then the other two fastened their attention on him and he told his story, stranger by far than either of theirs.

"And after that dreadful night with the takgabbi, did you have any trouble getting the girl for your wife?" questioned Zong-Teg.

"No, it all worked out easily and beautifully," replied the middle son with a smile. "You see, we loved each other. Nothing is impossible where love is."

"And—and—is she worth it? Have you won *your* heart's desire?" asked Zong-Yong with just a touch of envy in his voice.

Zong-Og had come unattended to the meeting of the three. He was simply dressed in the ordinary white linen of a Korean gentleman. One could see he was not rich and surely he was not famous, for the world had never heard of him. But there was about him an air of tranquillity and of quiet content. He drew his long slender white pipe from his mouth and held it in his fingers, smiling at the two.

"Yes, my brothers," said he, nodding his head several times by way of emphasis, "she is all that I dreamed and more; beautiful to look at, gay, kind, intelligent, an affectionate wife and a tender mother to my children. But if she were none of these she would still fulfill my heart's desire." He hesitated for a moment, looking at their questioning faces. "Because," he finished simply, "you see, just because I love her."

A NOTE ON SOURCE MATERIAL

BEFORE Columbus discovered America scholars in Korea were interested in collecting and recording native tales and folklore. A very distinguished gentleman named Yi-Ryuk wrote down some of them as early as 1465, and some two centuries later a famous and learned student who went by the delightful name of Im Bang gathered and set down more. These have been translated into English by James S. Gale in *Korean Folk Tales: Imps, Ghosts and Fairies* (Dutton, 1913). Other collections of age-old stories have drifted in to us from the long isolated and little known "hermit" nation and offer a fascinating study of comparative folklore as well as source material for children's stories. Among those that I have found particularly useful are:

Contes Coréens, compiled by A. Garine; adapted by Serge Persky (Paris: Delagrave, 1925).

Corea, The Hermit Nation, by William Elliot Griffis (New York: Charles Scribner's Sons, 1907).

Folk Tales from Korea, collected and translated by Zong In-Sob (London: Routledge and Kegan Paul, 1952).

Korean Fairy Tales, by William Elliot Griffis (New York: Thomas Y. Crowell Co., 1922).

Korean Tales; being a Collection of Stories Translated from the Korean Folk Lore, by Horace Newton Allen (New York: G. P. Putnam's Sons, 1889).

Koreans and Their Culture, The, by Cornelius Osgood (New York: Ronald Press Co., 1951).

Tales from Korea, by Young Tai Pyun (Seoul: International Cultural Association of Korea, 1948).

Things Korean, by Horace Newton Allen (New York: F. H. Revill Co., 1908).

To all of these books I am indebted for whatever background of Korean life I have got into my tales, and also for the threads of the stories themselves. These I have sometimes chosen from among several variants, changed, elaborated, combined with others, and given a dramatic build-up to interest modern children. Sometimes the foundation of the story has been merely a suggestive custom or tradition, but I have tried to keep it true to Korean thought.

The genuine folk tales as recorded by scholars, anthropologists, folklorists and such, are usually crude, unemotional, and lack the atmosphere and dramatic emphasis to appeal to a child. Yet in them so often lie seeds of beauty and delight and universal meaning! Therein lies the fun of trying to retell and reconstruct them, keeping the original background and foundation and "heading up" the suspense, excitement and meaning in them.

I hope very much that I have been able to do this successfully with these old Korean stories, for they seem to me to shed a clear and rather lovely light on the nature of the people for and with whom we have made common cause now for so long.

The culture of the Koreans is so very old, yet how little

we have known about it! Very noticeable in their native stories are gentleness, kindliness and a love of beauty. So many of their tales have a setting of gorgeous mountains and waterfalls and green forests! So many record adventures in an imagined spirit-world so beautiful it can only be suggested, not really described. Spirits and ghosts and goblins are for the most part either lovely and ethereal creatures, or amusing, or perhaps spine-prickling ones, but rarely horrible. One feels that a gentle, lovable people must have imagined these tales. And if the stories in this book awaken interest and friendliness and admiration in my young readers for those faraway people of "the Land of the Morning Calm," as the working over them has awakened in me, I shall be more than satisfied.

Eleanore M. Jewett